CHRISTMAS CRUSH

BRYNN NORTH

1

MARIA

"Come again!" I lied cheerfully, my best retail smile plastered across my face as I escorted the woman out the door, barely dodging the big shopping bag with the name *Bon Marche* she swung merrily. I watched with an attentive eye through the window until she was safely out of earshot.

"She better not come in again. Ever. Three hours and only spent a hundred bucks? I need a drink. Stat." I grabbed my pink water bottle and started gulping as my best and pretty much only friend, Luci, eyed me cautiously. She had stopped by during her Christmas shopping, and I was hoping I'd get a break in between customers to actually catch up with her.

"What's in that thing, spiked eggnog? Cuz if it is, I'm going to look up the number for AA. It's only two in the afternoon."

"On the first Saturday in December," I retorted, wishing that it was, in fact, eggnog in my water bottle and not just water mixed with a fruit punch flavored enhancer. I peered at the bottle a little more closely. Maybe it *would* taste okay with a shot of rum, sort of like a spiked punch bowl at a college frat party…it would certainly make work today more palatable.

"Stop it," Luci said firmly, shaking her head at me, making her blonde ponytail swing. Her blue eyes narrowed as she scanned me suspiciously. "I know what you're thinking. And you need to wait until five, like the rest of us."

I considered this for a moment, then decided she was probably right. "Working at a rich people's shop is so hard around Christmas. I'm run ragged trying to make everything perfect for them and get my own stuff done, too. You don't even want to hear about my to-do list for school," I whined instead. A full-time job plus full-time school meant a full-time mood. Add in the holidays, and I was getting crushed by my responsibilities while I wanted nothing more than to take a nap. If I had time for a nap, that is.

At those words, Luci instantly seemed to be interested in the pile of red scarves with snowflakes and fuzzy socks in front of her. A little *too* interested. I immediately grew suspicious. Luci never wore scarves. I knew this for a fact. I'd been helping Luci pick out all her clothes ever since the day she stepped foot into the store two years ago. I tried more than once to get Luci to accessorize but failed. She claimed she choked every time she wore a scarf, even in the freezing Minnesota weather. I suspected she'd been hanged or something in a previous life because *nobody* was too choked to not bundle up in the temperatures we got every year.

I stomped over to the fitting room, past the white sparkly Christmas tree I put up a few weeks ago, to where the woman left a three-foot pile of rejected clothing that was going to take me at least an hour to sort through and hang back up. Two hours, if it got busy again, which seeing that Christmas was only three weeks away, was more than likely to happen any minute now.

"Luciiiii," I said in a sing-song voice as I channeled my inner John Lennon, hoping that singing might put me in a holiday mood. It didn't work. Maybe I needed to switch to something more festive, like the Bieb's Christmas album, though I had a hunch Luci would run straight out of the store if I did that. But there was clearly something on her mind and I had to get to the bottom of it. "I have three finals, a term paper, and an entire portfolio of recommendation letters and project examples to get ready for in the next month. Not to mention a job in a retail store. At *Christmastime*. Spit it out because I don't have time for bull crap."

Luci turned around so fast I almost got secondhand whiplash. I didn't trust the sly expression on her face and I narrowed my eyes at her.

"You need recommendation letters and project examples?" Luci echoed, dropping the scarf she held. "For your PhD application?"

"Yes...why?" My voice trailed off, and I blinked. Luci knew what I needed for my application. Always had. I had been working on finishing my master's degree and aimed to get into the school's PhD program for as long as we had known each other. I cast an eye on Mount Discard and, giving up, headed to my phone. To get through the rest of the pile, I was going to require some serious help of the caffeinated variety. I pulled up the app for Starbucks and started punching in my order. "What do you want?"

"Well, I need help with—"

"No, to *drink*." I held up the phone and waved it at her. "But now I'm intrigued. And in a bad way."

"You're ordering from the bar? I didn't even know you could do that," Luci gasped. "Oh my God. Did you really develop a drinking problem? Is school getting you down that bad?" Luci was already on her phone. By the way she was frantically punching at the screen, I suspected she was searching Yelp reviews for the best rehab in the city.

"Quit being so dramatic," I demanded. "I'm ordering coffee. Not coffee martinis."

Luci's face immediately brightened, and she dropped her phone back in her purse. I knew it. "You're getting us Starbucks? Nice. I want a peppermint mocha."

"Don't thank me too much. You gotta pick it up and the crowds will be crazy. But I have better things to do." I nodded to the pile of clothes waiting for me as I finished up our order. I added an extra big tip, feeling sorry for the throngs of mall shoppers the baristas had to deal with. "Now spit it out."

"IneedyourhelpatEastVillage." Luci said it in a rush. I had to strain to decipher her word vomit.

"Wait, did you say you needed *help?*"

Luci volunteered at the East Village Senior Living Center and loved it. While I applauded her efforts, I didn't have a second to spare to do any volunteering. Something that Luci should know. I was bogged down with school and work the way it was. I let out a short sigh, thinking of some of my fellow students my age. Unlike most of them, I plotted out every dime and hour I had, needing to stay on top of my game to keep my scholarship and pay my bills. I couldn't even imagine having some mysterious benefactor referred to as "dad" who paid things like rent or tuition. Usually, I was fending off my mother's requests for 'just a few bucks' to tide her over until the next payday, which rarely came since she was too busy getting fired to maintain a stable job. I often wished I had one extra paycheck. One cushion to help me not be so nervous at the end of every month when the bills were due.

Luci started pacing, and I started wishing that the coffee could be delivered via drone. Intravenously would be even better.

"Yes. I need help organizing Santa for Seniors this year. I want to make it bigger and better than last year's party. I'd love to see a season-long event, since winter is so depressing, especially for older folks. I'm thinking of an outreach program to help out in the community throughout the season. It'll take a lot of work."

I was already backing up toward Mount Discard, hands held in front of me. "Oh, no. I admire what you're doing, but count me out. I don't have the time. Too much to do." I gestured to the pile behind me. "Starting with this." I felt bad for older folks in senior centers and all, with limited things to do, but I didn't have space to help.

"That's unfortunate," Luci said craftily, and for the second time since she stepped inside the boutique, my suspicion rose. "Because the center director loved the idea and told me since it's such an extensive project that there would be a stipend in it for someone to develop it. A thousand bucks, I think. I don't really need the money, now that I moved in with Alex, and you'd probably do a better job anyway, being that you're a soon-to-be psychologist doc and all. I wonder if the director would even give you a good letter of recommendation. You never know...and I guess we never will."

With a saucy wink, Luci ran out the door to pick up our drinks. For the second time in less than half an hour, I stared at someone leaving the store.

"*Oh noooo.*"

2

GABRIEL

"I brought bread, both white and wheat, and those frosted sugar cookies you like. Just hide them from the doctor this time, 'kay? Last thing we need is for her to get after us again for you sneaking in more sugar than you should."

"If she knew my grandson trained under one of the best bakers in France, she'd be stealing them from me. How much do you charge for them in your bakery again? Two bucks each?"

"Three," I said distractedly as I looked out into the snowy evening, watching a light flurry dance in the streetlights, only paying attention when Grandpa let out a sharp whistle.

"Three bucks for a cookie. Crazy." Grandpa shook his white hair in amazement and gave me a shrewd side-eye through his round wire-rimmed glasses. "You know, maybe I *should* leave some out tomorrow. Dr. Hernandez is young and cute—"

"And that'd be a *no* from me, dawg," I said firmly, emulating my favorite *American Idol* judge. The last thing I needed was Grandpa lining up women waiting for me when I came by for one of my frequent visits. And I was pretty sure that the last thing his doctor wanted was potential dates set up for her when she was trying to do her job. "Besides. She came into the bakery last week. With her *girlfriend*."

Grandpa crossed his arms in front of his chest and gave me a stern look from where I sat in his favorite leather armchair. "First, Randy Jackson hasn't been on *American Idol* since 2013. Second, the revival on ABC is horrible. Third, the best star that came out of that show was Carrie Underwood. Fourth—"

I stretched my hands above my head, thinking I may as well get comfortable. It was my own fault for being stupid enough to bring up Grandpa's favorite show. Grandpa watched every season of *American Idol* since the first, and even had a little betting pool going on with a few of his buddies at East Village, the senior living center they lived in. They invited me to join, but after winning three years in a row, my invitation seemed mysteriously lost in the mail for the following season.

"Fourth what?" I asked wearily. It probably had to do with the live concert tours being subpar. I knew this too, since I was the one recruited to go with Grandpa every time they came through town. I'd never admit it, but my favorite year was when Sanjaya was on tour.

"Fourth is that you need to move on already," Grandpa said, jarring me out of my mental ranking of the best *American Idol* concerts. My head whipped toward him. Grandpa *never* moved on from the topic of *American Idol* this fast. He really must be passionate about me needing to move on. Bad news for me. "Fine. Don't date Dr. Hernandez. But I'm guessing Amanda came in again today?"

I started to carefully examine Grandpa's Christmas tree, pulling out a few loose needles and rearranging his ornaments by color.

"Quit evading the question," he ordered.

I wondered what it was like to have a Grandpa that took you

fishing instead of giving interrogations about your love life. "How'd you know?"

"Forty-seven years in psychology is how I knew. You've been in a pissy mood ever since you walked in."

I considered arguing that I wasn't in a pissy mood but immediately decided against it. I'd never convince Grandpa, who, to his point, spent almost thirty years as a private practice psychologist before teaching at the university. He even made it up to the dean of the department before retirement.

"Yes," I replied simply, letting Grandpa take what he wanted out of that one word, figuring he may as well put that psychologist's mind of his to good use and all. Knowing him, he was already examining it from no less than three angles.

"Tell her not to come into the bakery. Text it to her so she knows to leave you alone."

"You make it sound so simple. I can't kick out a paying customer," I defended myself, even though I couldn't quite figure out why. I grimaced over the memory of Amanda's syrupy sweet voice today, asking how Grandpa Paul was doing. As if she truly cared. Amanda, one of the fakest people I had ever met, only cared about climbing the city's social ladder, going to the best parties, and wearing the sexiest clothes. Too bad it took me over a year to figure it out. Thinking with the wrong head, as Grandpa put it. Grandpa had known it from the start, and only I was surprised when Amanda dumped me for a fancier model. I had been heartbroken at the time and vowed the next woman I dated would be completely different. Too bad it was hard to find her. Unless my next girlfriend appeared in front of me, like a mirage or the ghost of Christmas Yet to Come. Though now that I thought about it, that wasn't a good thing, right? The Ghost of Christmas Yet to Come was the scary guy. Well. Seemed to sum up my love life about right.

Grandpa made a *pfft* noise. "The heck you can't. You own the place, don't you? You get to decide who comes through the doors. Not her. You're not being assertive enough."

At least I got my professional advice free, even if it did come with the painful price of being unsolicited and relentlessly followed up on.

"I gotta go. Need to start some cakes for this weekend." My croquembouche and bûche de Noël were my signature pieces around the holidays, and orders were piling in all month long. Owning the highest rated bakery in the city was no joke around the holidays, and I pretty much worked non-stop in December, but I hoped if I got ahead by stocking my walk-in freezer I might fend off some desperate people this week. Crazy how many sob stories I heard about how their Christmas celebration would be ruined if they didn't have the exact baked good they wanted. I was always tempted to ask them what they thought about a genuine crisis, like landmines in Cambodia, if not having poached pears on the table was worthy of their panic, but I was smart enough not to say it out loud.

"I'll see you in a few days, okay?" I said instead of answering him. I pointed my electric start button out the window toward my car, and with a quick hug to Grandpa, headed out the door.

I paused before the front door in the lobby, taking a moment to zip up my jacket before plunging into the wintry night. Just as I reached for the handle, it opened with a force, blowing frigid cold air straight at me.

"Whoa," I said reflexively, stopping so I didn't plow the woman down with the door by pushing it right back at her. Then, as I saw why I was blocked, I repeated the word and stepped backward.

Whoa.

Thankfully, this time it was only in my head. The woman I almost hit with the door had long black hair that cascaded in curls down to the middle of her back, a shapely figure, and the widest brown eyes I had ever seen. I spent months searching for the best chocolate for my ganache, going through what seemed like hundreds to find the right one, and working on getting it melted just right to display a gorgeous shade of deep shiny brown on my cakes. And now I knew all that was a waste of time because one glance at this woman's eyes and I knew what color I should have been aiming for all along. Trailing my gaze down further, my eyes took in the tight skinny jeans that showed off every curve she had and her fashionable high-heeled boots.

Nope. I definitely wouldn't push a woman like this out of anywhere. I paused for a second time as a blonde woman rushed in behind her, and they scurried down the hall.

"Thanks," the brunette said, and I realized that all the movies were wrong. This was what Christmas angels sounded like. I thought about faking some excuse to follow the two women, but the click-clacking heels of the brunette's boots meant business. The prospect of getting sprayed by bear spray for acting like a creeper was a deterrent as well.

Instead, I took one last glimpse at her bouncing black curls and with an internal sigh of regret, turned toward the door.

3

MARIA

"So, what do you think?" I prayed that Simon, the director of East Village, would like my proposal. Beads of sweat formed under my sweater as he flicked through the papers I placed in front of him a few minutes previously. I tried to take an inconspicuous sniff, wondering if I was starting to smell. *Nope.* Not yet at least, though my favorite striped sweater was probably going to need a good dry cleaning. Something I usually tried to avoid spending money on. Too bad most of the fancy designer clothes—purchased from my store's clearance rack using my generous employee discount—required such care.

Simon nodded slowly, raising my hopes through my chest all the way to the ceiling. Getting this project would be a major boost, not only to my portfolio but also to my budget. After a quick meeting with him a few days ago to go over requirements, I labored for hours, designing a program to keep seniors active and engaged in the community to alleviate their boredom and the winter doldrums. I imagined putting smiles on the senior's faces, and it uplifted my own spirits. If the plain office with the white walls and basic black chairs was any indication, this was a dull place.

I looked out the window while I waited for Simon to speak. Five at night and the sky was dark. No wonder people became depressed in the winter. Nothing to do. I vowed to change that if I landed the assignment. I had googled ideas and designed all sorts of potential program plans and ended up pretty pleased with some of my work.

Simon kept flipping through the pages of my portfolio, and moisture under my armpits grew until a bead of sweat trickled down my side. I was torn between wanting this job desperately and worried about the hours it would take to create the program. Adding this to my schedule would put me practically at my edge. But all the same, I was grateful Luci gave me the opportunity instead of keeping it for herself.

Any self-help book would promise a miracle cure to reduce stress, involving reducing caffeine intake, meditating for hours a day, and lighting incense that envoked the smell of a fresh rain shower in the hills of Peru or some bullcrap like that. But I knew they were wrong. The only way to reduce your stress was to chase after my dreams like I was chasing after David Beckham in his Calvin Kleins holding a cupcake. Relentlessly.

After about a thousand years, Simon finally spoke. "I think we can make this work. You obviously have a great eye for this type of thing. We may need to tweak the activities a bit, if you don't mind. But winter is rough for many people here, so I want to give them something to look forward to."

"*Yes!*" I had to restrain myself from jumping up and kissing the man on top of his bald head. Visions started flashing before my eyes. Not visions like I was dying. More like future visions. The Ghost of Christmas Yet to Come came for me, but this time he wasn't scary. He brought me visions of paid cell phone bills, grocery bags with more than cereal and milk in them, and maybe even a few bucks set aside in my savings account. I loved my version of this ghost. He was my buddy. I mean, sure, this would bring a lot of work, but I'd have to manage somehow. Growing up in my family required me to be fast, savvy, and hardworking. Even in high school, I put in over thirty hours a week at the local department store in addition to getting straight As. Had to if I wanted a way out. This would be the same.

I hoped, at least.

I shot out my hand to Simon, and after a brief moment of hesitation, he shook it. As soon as his hand hit mine in a clammy greeting, I groaned internally. No wonder he hesitated. *Great job grossing the dude out, Maria.* My hand had gone all sweaty with anticipation, and I noticed Simon discreetly wipe his palm off on his pants as he stood up. Would it be embarrassing to offer him the anti-bacterial hand gel? Or polite? I mean, I'd want some, but then again, it might make an awkward situation even worse. Like, what could I say? *Sorry I dripped sweat all over you, here's something to clean up the germs?* Better not, I decided. That'd just bring more attention to a nasty situation.

"Are we getting started now?" I prodded, wondering if that's why he rose out of his chair. The faster I got started, the faster the money would hit my bank account. Tuition was coming up in January, and Christmas was around the corner. My mom would expect my usual Christmas card full of cash, in addition to the big bottle of knock-off Grey Goose that I got for her at Costco every year. Sometimes I didn't even know why I bothered with the money. I should cut to the chase and get a few more bottles of vodka and toss in some scratch-off lottery tickets. Save my mom a trip to the store and all.

Simon laughed. "Guess you're eager."

"I'm just excited to help people out," I said, trying to calm my voice down. It wasn't entirely untrue. I was also enthusiastic about the paycheck.

He checked his watch. "I need to get going to my Friday night grilling class, but let's go meet someone I think will be interested in helping us spearhead this program."

Grilling class? In ten degrees? What was it with men who loved grilling so much they needed to do it in the dead of winter? I decided not to ask because I'd never understood, anyway. Instead, I followed Simon down the hall, glancing through the doors as I wove through the halls after him. We passed a library with leather-bound books and comfortable chairs, and a theater room with a leather recliners. To my right, I saw several people having a conversation around a roaring fireplace, and to the left a fitness center, where an older man was running on a treadmill, easily beating my personal record. Not that it was a particularly high bar.

My gaze drifted around, and my stomach sank as I realized this was a lot different from the senior center I remembered visiting my grandma at before she died. I wondered why Luci didn't tell me how hip this place was. Or did she, and I had a mental block on what I thought a senior center looked like. I wondered if my activities, such as game nights and tai chi, would be well received.

Simon led us over to an older woman in a wheelchair. "Hi Molly, have you seen Paul? He's usually playing piano around now, isn't he?"

"I saw him leave ten minutes ago. He said something about going to the south rooftop to meet his grandson for a cocktail."

My mouth hung open. *Fitness center? Piano? Rooftop bar?* Yep. I didn't have to question any longer if my activities were on the lame side. They were. I cringed as I followed Simon to the elevators where, after a short ride, we stepped out into a large loft-style room. To my left, a group of people gathered at a shuffleboard table. An older woman held court at a bar area to the right, with three men clustered around her, laughing at a story she told. Must have been quite a wild one too, the way all eyes were on her. That, or she was single and they were competing for her attention. My eyes got wider and wider as I took in the room, gaping at the best feature, which was an entire wall of floor-to-ceiling glass windows. Small groups of people gazed out into the snowy evening and toward the roaring outdoor fire pit. Classic Christmas music played over the speakers, reminding us to have a Holly Jolly Christmas.

Can I be old? Like right now? I thought wildly. This place was about ten times more exciting than my average weekend. Heck, make that fifteen, as I noticed a pool table in the corner. My mind flashed to the proposal I felt so proud about, and I felt like running out of the room. The entire East Village Outreach proposal centered on assuming older people were bored and needed something to do. By the looks of it, they did perfectly fine entertaining themselves. A lot better than I entertained myself. My Friday night usually consisted of popcorn and a bottle of cheap wine while I studied.

"Ah, there's Paul. Let's go talk to him. He'll be a great ally to rouse people up and get them interested in your program. He knows everyone here." I followed Simon's glance to the two people playing pool. One was a distinguished-looking older gentleman, but it was the person next to him that stopped me short.

"Is that—?" I gasped, staring at the stranger in front of me. No way. It couldn't be. My heart pulsed wildly, and despite my long day between school and work, my tiredness evaporated and I was wide awake.

"Yes, that's Paul and his grandson, Gabriel. Wonderful people," Simon noted, striding forward.

My heart slowed down to a reasonable pace. *Of course Ryan Reynolds wouldn't be here, in a senior living complex in Minnesota,* I admonished myself. That was silly. Though, upon further examination, it was entirely plausible that a man who looked just like Ryan Reynolds, with the added bonus of being closer to my age, was located in such a place. My brain screeched at me. DANGER ZONE. DO NOT LOOK AGAIN. DO NOT PASS GO. I was okay with the idea of collecting two hundred bucks, though.

But I was here to do a job, and that was that, so like a good girl, I listened to my brain and ignored Ryan Reynolds Jr, and followed Simon to the pool table.

4
GABRIEL

I drew back and hit the cue ball neatly, sending the red ball ricocheting off the side and into the corner pocket. I grinned at Grandpa triumphantly.

"Lucky shot," Grandpa groused, chalking his cue stick. "But don't forget, I've been doing this since before you were born."

I was about to retort back that experience didn't equal expertise when I noticed Simon heading our way and lost all words. Not because of him. Simon was a good guy and all, but he wasn't exactly my type. It was who trailed behind him. The brunette from a few days ago. The one that made me stop her from getting hit with the door, then stopped me in my tracks with her gorgeous curves. I thought she was beautiful then, but I was wrong. Now that I saw her closer, she was drop-dead gorgeous.

"You set this up," I accused Grandpa in a whisper as they approached. I didn't know how he did it, but I'm sure his conniving mind came up with this scheme somehow. Maybe an early Christmas present? Not that I was arguing. Santa really nailed the ol' gift list this year.

"Quit your yapping. I had nothing to do with this." Grandpa

took a closer look. "Though if I were a smarter man, I would have."

Grandpa gave me a little shove, landing me directly in the woman's path. I felt the nudge of Grandpa's cue stick against the back of my tricep, prompting me to stretch out my arm to meet the woman's eagerly awaiting hand.

Grandpa was so going to hear about this later. Even if he didn't set this up, by his gleeful expression, he sure as heck was loving it. When my hand made contact with hers, the beating pulse roaring through my veins turned into a full-on tidal wave. Her hand was so soft and petite in mine that I felt an irrational need to protect it. Protect her. Which was stupid of me because one glance at this determined-looking woman indicated she had an aura that showed she was confident and capable. But still. Something in me wanted to wrap her up in a blanket, give her a cup of tea, and put on bad Hallmark Christmas movies while I baked her cookies.

With superhuman strength, I let go of her hand, noticing she wiped it off on her pants right after. I took a quick glance at my own palm, one that a mere second ago seemed like the gateway to my happiness. That traitor. Was it sweaty or gross? I didn't think so. Maybe she thought *I* was sweaty and gross? My heart sank. Great. It had been so long since I touched anyone besides customers at the cafe, handing out baked goods and their change, that I was disgusting and didn't even realize it.

But Christmas cookies never gave me this many sparks, not even chocolate-covered with sprinkles.

"To what do my wonderful grandson, head baker of Spruce Patisserie, and I owe you for the pleasure of this visit?" Grandpa's gracious question was directed at Simon, but his eyes were pointed at the woman, making sure she noticed what he said.

I glared at Grandpa. I was going to have to talk to him later about proper wingman skills. Not that I wanted any help myself, but if Grandpa was trying to hook up any of his widow friends with any women around this joint, I would need to teach him to be a little more subtle.

The woman in front of him spoke, and I got lost for a minute, watching her bright red lipstick flash across her face instead of listening to her words.

Wake up, dude. She already thinks you're gross. If she can't even take your hand sweat, she sure as heck isn't going to sign up for your kissing germs. Even a longer shot. I forced myself to pay attention to what she was saying. Something about a program?

"Yes, we are looking for seniors who get cabin fever in the winter to help out around the community. Do things like tutor students, work with animal shelters, that type of thing."

Wow. What a wonderful endeavor. Minnesota winters dragged on for months, and even the most active of people fall victim to the winter blues. Having some way to feel active and helpful would be a major boost to this community. But still. My heart went out to her. She apparently hadn't figured out yet this was this hottest senior spot in the city, and they wanted to do more than play a few rounds of chess. Just the rumors about who was running around with another man behind their maybe-boyfriend's back while he was visiting his grandkids out of state could keep the gossips busy for hours. I knew because I was often asked to weigh in with my opinion of the modern dating world. Hmmm...A thought crossed my mind. Maybe this gorgeous woman would like some help with the ideas? From a young, spry gentleman? Only to be polite, of course. Help her and the community out. Yep, that was me, Mr. Helpful.

Simon leaned up against the pool table, and the sparkly paper snowflakes hanging from the ceiling danced merrily above our heads. "I thought of you, Paul. You always like a little community service. Thought maybe you'd like to work with this lady to raise awareness in our center. Get people rallied up."

I ignored the massive grin spreading across Grandpa's face. It was already my busy season. I didn't know if I had time for Grandpa's matchmaking, too. Then I snuck one more glance at her and knew I didn't stand a chance. For a woman like this, I'd make the time. I'd stay up late and drink 5-Hour Energy shots to stay awake at work the next day. heck, I'd have cases of Red Bull auto-shipped to me on a weekly basis.

"We'd love to help." Grandpa threw his arm around my shoulder. "Why don't we head over to the tables and discuss it over a drink?"

Subtle, Grandpa, real subtle.

Before I knew what was happening, Simon was saying his goodbyes, and I was being propelled to a small table near the window with a perfect view of the fire and city below us. My suspicions grew even more when the woman sat down, and I realized the small table only had *two* chairs.

"I'll go grab us a bottle of wine to share," Grandpa announced as he beelined straight past the bar toward the corner where I knew he kept his favorite bottles in his wine locker.

With Grandpa on his mission, we sat in awkward silence. I racked my brain for something, anything to say, but the pounding in my chest made it impossible to think. "So, uh, my name is Gabriel," I said, grimacing on how lamely that came out. Well. At least it was half a step up from sitting in silence.

"Maria," the woman next to me answered and smiled. Along with that smile, the heavens opened up and angels started to sing. Sounded just like her, too. Before I could calm my racing heart, Grandpa reappeared with a bottle of wine. I snuck a glance at the label and was tempted to bury my head in my hands. Grandpa had pulled out his *special occasion* label. The expensive label he usually reserved for retirements and graduations, and apparently for when he was trying to help his grandson woo a beautiful woman.

After I drank this amazing bottle with this gorgeous woman, that is.

Grandpa slapped his forehead with the back of his hand, trying to act casual but failing miserably. Hope he didn't have *win an Emmy award* on his bucket list. "I just realized that I have, umm...something downstairs in my apartment that I needed to get."

Oh, he wasn't going to get off this easily. "What did you forget, Grandpa?" I asked innocently as he handed me a wine opener.

"The...thing," he said, drawing out the word.

Maria blinked. "The...thing?"

"You'll have to forgive Grandpa. He's getting a little old," I apologized to her as I hurriedly moved my ankle away from the kick Grandpa was aiming in its direction.

He scowled at me behind Maria's back. "Yes, I do believe that's what I forgot. The thing. Why don't you two settle in, and I'll be right back?"

Grandpa didn't even wait for an answer before he was gone. I kinda had to admire how fast a seventy-three-year-old man could move when he felt the need to. I glanced over at Maria's puzzled face. Well, we may as well make the best of it. I had a feeling that it would take him a while to find "the thing."

"Wine?" I asked, reaching for her glass.

5

MARIA

I took a sip of the wine that the young Ryan Reynolds—excuse me, *Gabriel*—offered me. This was a bit of an awkward moment, but hopefully, Paul would be back soon and we could have a talk about the next steps. I'd have to find a chair for him, though. But really. Of all people in the world, did I really need to be left with a man who had tousled blonde hair, impish good looks, and a slight smattering of freckles under that minor scruff of his? Being left with The Grinch would have been so much easier.

"So, Gabriel, you visit your Grandpa often?" I forced out, not sure what else to say. I mean, I know what I wanted to say. I wanted to ask all sorts of things, like what's your full name, date of birth, zodiac sign, address, and especially, what is your phone number? But I was going to say none of those things, because getting entangled with a stranger was the very last thing I needed on my to-do list.

"Yep." He smiled fondly, and I found myself smiling back at the obvious love he had for his grandfather. "He's the only family I have around here since my parents and sisters moved to Illinois after I graduated high school." He slid his phone out of his pocket and showed me the screen saver. On it was a beautiful family, all mugging for the camera. Two parents stood in the back, showing the city behind them. Gabriel and three equally blonde sisters, who I guessed to be around sixteen, stood in front of them. One glance at the photo, and you could tell they were a tight-knit, loving family. A pang went through my heart, and I wondered how nice it would be to have a close family. One that checked in on you instead of checking in on how much you had to spare in your bank account.

"Are they...?" I started looking at the picture more closely.

"Yep. Triplets." He grinned, tapping at the screen. "Triple the sisters, triple the trouble."

Dang. Would the picture-perfect family life of this guy never end? The next thing he'd tell me was they had a family collie named Lassie. What would he think of my family? People with families like his never understood families like mine. Sure, they might sympathize a little, throw a few well-meaning suggestions my way, but they never truly understood what it was like to have a mom who charged you rent starting at fifteen years old and hadn't cooked you dinner since you were six. Why it was easier to keep your distance by pretending you were perpetually busy, instead of talking on the phone five times a week.

He took a sip of wine, then put the glass down. "Can't have too much of this stuff. Too many very early mornings for me, getting up and opening the bakery and all. Seems like work, work, work."

Disappointment shot through me, but I quickly determined it wasn't disappointment after all. It was relief. Simple misunderstanding. I had too much going on to be *interested* in a man, especially one that was crazy busy, too. I couldn't even imagine trying to solve the math equation that would inevitably be our schedules. I didn't need a romance. If there was one thing I learned growing up in my family, I needed stability. I was nobody's gold digger, but there was a reason I worked so hard in college, all the way up to my PhD application. Sure, I loved psychology. But I also loved the idea of security and a career that could pull in a good salary. I was done with a lifestyle of crappy apartments, revolving stepdads, and iffy paychecks that didn't quite cover the bills. I fought my way out of that life when I was seventeen, and dang it, it was going to stay that way.

Yep. Guys like Gabriel are trouble. Sexy, dangerous trouble. A distraction from my goals, and there was no way I was going to put up with that.

I diverted my eyes from Mr. Trouble and started to scan the massive loft-style room we were in, full of life and excitement. I sensed Gabriel's gaze on me, and a flush crept up my cheeks. I looked up to catch his eyes and tried to ignore the way my heart skipped a beat at the amusement I saw in them.

"Nice place, huh? Makes me want to be old. Seems like college students and senior centers have it about right. Living in a big fun community. Sure beats boring apartments."

"I was just thinking the same thing earlier!" I exclaimed, and suddenly this awkward moment between two strangers cracked open into one of comradery. "I'm kind of nervous about this program I'm supposed to develop, though. I went on Pinterest and searched for activities for seniors. But these people are more exciting than me. I don't think they're going to be into Bingo or board game nights like Pinterest led me to believe." I silently cursed Luci for not telling me she volunteered at the coolest senior center in the world. Surely, she could have slipped that tidbit in at some point?

Gabriel laughed. A sexy, deep laugh. It sent every nerve ending I had, and some I didn't realize existed, dancing. "Yeah. These people are pretty hip. But don't get the wrong idea. They get bored and lonely, too." He nodded to a woman in the corner with pink streaks in her gray hair. "Lori over there gets so bored that she cycles through new boyfriends every three months. I'm not supposed to say anything, but apparently, the nurses have to remind her about the rising cases in STDs amongst seniors."

I widened my eyes. "Is that seriously a thing going on in here?" I glanced around, more inquisitive this time, trying to imagine the comings and goings of these people. Whoa. Two women tried to catch the eye of a man standing by the window, failing. A couple whispered and giggled quietly as they watched the cold winter night. Looks like I was out of the loop when it came to older people's dating lives. Or anyone's, really.

Gabriel lowered his voice. "Look at Marien over there. She hits on Grandpa all the time. I think it drives her crazy that he won't agree to a date. But he refuses to do it."

I got a little sappy-eyed at the idea of his grandpa not wanting to date. True love did exist, even if I had never seen it. "Oh, does he miss your grandma too much?"

Gabriel snorted. "Probably not. They had been divorced for years before she died. He doesn't like how Marien's last three husbands died of mysterious causes and doesn't want to be next."

Oh.

Gabriel stretched his arm out, and my heart momentarily stopped. Was he going to put it around the back of my chair like my middle school boyfriend did to be slick at the movies? Wasn't he a little too old for that? Did I want him to perform such a gesture? *YES* my heart screamed at the same time my mind screamed *NO*. My panic melted when I saw he was reaching to move a chair out of someone's way so they could get by in their wheelchair. Stupid me for getting so caught up in things.

"You know," he said abruptly. "I could help you come up with ideas. Since I've been around here more, visiting Grandpa. I can give you an idea of what they might like to do. We could meet up and talk over dinner?"

Oh no. I wasn't going to fall for this trap, even if it was with Ryan Reynolds Junior. "I don't date," I said stiffly. Better to set him straight.

His eyes flashed in amusement. "Never?"

I shook my head firmly, avoiding his hazel eyes that wanted me to say yes. "Never. No time for dating, especially in December. I'm a grad student at the U, and it's way too stressful. Finals are rough, remember?"

"I wouldn't know because I didn't go to college."

"Just trust me on that," I said, not wanting to dive into it. "It's a life of work, study, and if you're lucky enough to be able to after all that stress, sleep."

"Well, you gotta eat, don't you?" His sly tone showed me he was taking this as a challenge.

I twirled a strand of hair around my finger. My heart started racing, but I wasn't sure why. Maybe it was the dim lighting and the way he was so close I could see the flecks of black in those hazel eyes. "Yes," I admitted. "But usually I grab a granola bar or something on the fly."

"That's not nutritious." He made a little *tsk tsk* sound.

Wait a minute. What made him the expert here? "You're a baker, that's not exactly nutritious either!" I exclaimed.

He nodded slowly. "You're right. Seems like we both need to work on our nutrition. Take it a little more seriously, it sounds." He tapped his finger against his mouth like he was thinking, and I narrowed my eyes at his exaggeration. And tried not to look at his lips, which gave me thoughts that I didn't want to get into. Thoughts of mistletoe, kissing, and how soft those lips would feel against mine.

"You know The Fish Bar?" He waited for my nod. Of course I knew The Fish Bar. I had never been, being that it was the opposite of cheap, but the modern, all-glass restaurant downtown was hard to miss. "It has good salmon. We could increase our Omega 3 intake. Make our primary care doctors proud."

I evaluated this for a moment. I mean, Omega 3 was important, right? Even though it seemed like an odd conversation topic. But still. "Couldn't we just take fish oil supplements?"

He shook his head and rubbed his chin. "I went to culinary school, remember? I learned about nutrition, at least a little. Whole foods are best. Not supplements. I have a moral obligation to keep you healthy now that I know you exist on packaged food and vitamins." He leaned closer. Conspiratorially. I tried to ignore his scent, which was a mixture of cinnamon and nutmeg. Made sense, since he was a baker. Made me wonder if his lips tasted the same. "But I *assure* you, this is not a date. Just want to keep you healthy."

Hmmm. Hard to argue with that point. People needed vitamins... "Fine," I finally agreed, figuring out a loophole. "But we meet on a weeknight."

He looked bemused. "Like a Tuesday? Won't even give me a weekend?"

I shook my head, eyes determined. "Nope. Weekend nights are date nights. This is not a date. This is...sharing a meal. For nutritional purposes, of course. And we meet there. No picking me up. Picking me up is a date."

He gazed at the window in front of us before giving me a sly look. "Okay. I agree. We'll mutually share a table at our non-date. Gotcha. But what if..."

He bit his lip and gave a slow, short shake of his head, pausing so long that pins and needles started growing in my butt. "If what?" I finally barked out.

He put a finger on his strong jawline and gave it a few taps, giving me that impish grin I already seemed to know by heart. "You know. The Fish Bar is attached to the theater."

I knew that, too. It was a gorgeous theater and showcased the city's best plays. Not that I ever had time or money to see a play. I crossed my hands over my chest to hide my beating heart. "Your point?"

He crossed his, too, giving me a sneaky look. "What if...naw, that won't work."

"What won't?" He had me drawn in now. I was eager to figure out what wouldn't work.

"Well. What if I accidentally *found* tickets for *A Christmas Carol*?"

Despite my best efforts to keep it cool, excitement started to build in my chest. The theater's version of *A Christmas Carol* was legendary in the city. I had never been but had heard all about it. Had always wanted to go, but it was hardly something Mom would bring me to. When I was a kid, her idea of a holiday celebration was to find receipts flying around the parking lot and find the same item on the shelf to return it for cash. Holidays were the best time, she told me. Receipts were longer. I winced, remembering that particular Life Pro Tip. Going to a Christmas play would be a definite step up. *But*...there was one problem. No dating meant no dating. Buying tickets to a play would *definitely* be a date.

He took another sip of his wine, sneaking a glance at me as I pondered this for a second. I mean, finding tickets and letting them go unused would be wasteful, right? Suddenly, I wanted to have a carefree night. One where I could have dinner and a show instead of popcorn and homework. The closest I got was pizza and Netflix with Luci. Which I loved and all, but a girls' night was a little different from a night on the town. I wanted to feel like a normal, breezy girl without responsibilities and stress. One on the arm of a cute guy, going to a fabulous show. One night wouldn't kill me, would it?

"Well. If you found them, that's one thing. But buying is a date. So no buying."

"No buying?"

"No buying. Even my dinner." My voice was firm. I didn't want to be indebted to anyone, even a cute guy like this. I'd just have to ask for an extra shift or two at work to cover what I suspected would be a spendy piece of fish. If that was even possible with my schedule.

He winced. "But I have a gift card."

Really? They sold gift cards for one of the nicest restaurants in town? Did they *do* gift cards? By the way Gabriel was innocently taking a sip of wine, it was apparent he had no plans on telling me how he procured it.

"Fine." My voice was crisp, a total contrast to the gooey feeling in my stomach. That traitor. "I understand that a gift card shouldn't go to waste. But this is *not* a date."

A grin broke out across his face. *Dang it.* I was in for it now. "I can work with that. So. Sunday. Meet me at the theater for found tickets and a non-date meal. Let's shake on this business transaction."

I hesitated, then for the second time that night, shook his hand. Just like before, the heat of his palm went straight up to my arm and into my heart.

Now I had to find something to wear.

6
GABRIEL

"Hey, Grandpa, can you drop these on the floor?"

Grandpa glanced at the two pieces of paper I held out. "What in the heck you want me to do that for?"

I rolled my eyes. "So I can find them. Obviously."

"And here I thought I'd heard it all by now," he groused as he took the tickets out of my hand and dropped them on the floor between us. We watched them flutter to the carpet, like the snow fluttered outside in the cold afternoon.

June, who Grandpa referred to as his 'lady friend' but I referred to as his 'crush'—at least when she wasn't around—reached down to pick them up. "*A Christmas Carol,*" she read. "You bought paper tickets? What is this, 1995? Get their app like everyone else."

"Long story. I needed to have found them. Not bought them."

"Young people these days," Grandpa grumbled to June. "Always making things more complicated than they need to be."

I was already headed toward the door, having dropped off the treats I promised them. "Maria and I are going on a non-date. See ya later!"

"Wait!"

I turned as I tucked my scarf around my neck. The temp tonight would be no more than ten degrees, and the last thing I needed was frostbite.

"What is a 'non-date'?"

Dang it. I didn't want to get into that. I regretted not keeping my mouth shut. "We're meeting for a show and dinner. But it's not a date."

June stared at me and tilted her head. "But you're single. She's single. A show and dinner seems like a date."

"I don't disagree, but I gotta roll with it. She's a tough one." I smiled, remembering her feisty attitude. Somehow, instead of being a turnoff, her determination attracted me even more, even if I knew we both secretly knew it was a date. But, if that was the game she wanted to play, so be it. I also didn't exactly lie when I said I had a gift card. It just wasn't to The Fish Bar. My parents sent me a gift card to the Nike store for my birthday.

Maria should have asked for specifics if she really wanted to know.

"Don't forget to bring her something," Grandpa ordered. "Women like that sort of thing. Flowers or candy."

"Flowers will freeze while we eat. Besides, that's creepy, Grandpa. Women don't like that sort of thing these days."

June shook her head in disagreement. "It is not creepy. It'll set you apart."

I pondered their suggestion for a minute, wondering if they had a point. Even though Maria was adamant she didn't date, I had no doubt a woman like her had men chasing her all over town, and if it was a race, I was determined to end up with the gold medal. Last week during my visit, I had overheard Sandra from the fifth-floor talk about how her latest date from the SilverSingles app brought her some new compression socks she loved. I tried to think of someone closer to my age who had been on a date recently but only came up with one of my part-time bakery employees. Mykenna, my best high school employee, *did* tell me that her latest boyfriend of the week brought her a selfie mirror for her gym locker at school, and she loved it. Somehow, though, I thought Maria would consider both compression socks and a selfie mirror an insult.

Grandpa saw me ponder. "Get her something useful. Or pretty."

Way to be specific, Gramps. I glanced at the snow through the window behind him. I quickly punched in "best presents for graduate students" into Google. Grandpa watched as I did a rapid scroll through the ideas until I stopped at one in particular. *Huh.* Maybe this would work. I flashed them my phone.

"Oh, that's a good one." June giggled. "A blanket makes a woman think of the bedroom, which makes her think of--"

I cut her off before visualizations of what went on in her bedroom could seep into my brain. That was one piece of knowledge I could definitely live without. Needed to live without. Not to mention if I got Maria on that train of thought, she'd definitely think I was a creep.

"Love you, Gramps. See you next time."

"Text me all about it," I heard him call out as the door shut behind me.

I HAD JUST enough time to skid into the store before I met Maria at the theater for our date / non-date. I stopped short when I saw her waiting for me, not realizing I had been holding my breath. I thought she looked amazing at the East Village, but dressed up in a fuzzy red coat and matching hat made her look so adorable that I had to resist the urge to pull her into my arms to warm her up.

Instead, I held out the bag for her, living for the five seconds our fingers brushed as I transferred the handle over to her. Even through our layers of mittens, the heat from her fingers warmed my soul enough to feel like it was ninety-five degrees out, not five degrees. "This is for you."

She hesitantly took it, her arm dropping fast. "Whoa!" she yelped. "What's in this thing? A brick?"

I shoved my hands in my pocket as embarrassment flowed over me. Why did I ever listen to Grandpa and June? I knew she'd think a man bringing her a present on a first date was creepy. That piece of dating advice probably had been out of style since the 1950s. I cursed myself as she lifted a corner of the pink knit blanket out of the large bag.

Way to be a creeper, Gabriel.

"Is this a...?" Her mouth dropped open.

I shifted from one foot to another as my heart sank. This moment was about a thousand times more awkward than I thought it would be. Did I insult her that badly? She was an independent woman, that was clear, and maybe she assumed a man buying her something represented, I don't know, antifeminism instead of wanting to be nice.

I cleared my throat. "Yeah. A weighted blanket. You mentioned you were stressed and had trouble sleeping with school and all. Sleeping with a weighted blanket is supposed to help you fall asleep faster, and reduce stress and anxiety...and I got a knit one, thought it'd look nicer than a basic fuzzy one..."

I'll never, ever listen to June again, that's for sure. Next time I'd go straight for the compression socks. More neutral. Maria was probably going to slap me now for thinking of her in bed. Even though I quite liked the image.

My thoughts were drowned out in the scent of plum and honeysuckle as Maria threw her arms around me.

7

MARIA

I couldn't believe I let my guard down like this. This is the way people ended up in white murder vans. You start trusting someone, accept one little blanket, let your guard down a little, and next thing you know, you're six feet under in a field under the snow, right behind the best theater in town. I saw enough true crime stories. I knew how this stuff worked.

But the blanket might be worth it, I thought as I snuck my hand down to feel the fuzzy knit fabric as we sat in the dark theater. Stress was my middle name these days, with anxiety being my last. Anything that would take that down a notch would be a major relief. Not to mention that I usually saved a few bucks to buy myself a Christmas present each year, being that I was pretty much the only person who gave me one, besides Luci of course, and this year it wasn't going to happen. Just this morning, Mom called, asking for a few bucks to cover the electric bill. When I asked her why she hadn't asked my latest stepdad to chip in, she defended him as usual, telling me he was working on his latest startup and how it was going to make them millions. I tried to point out that, if after five years he still wasn't turning a profit, and in fact, was burning money at a rate that reminded me of the Joker in *The Dark Knight*, that it could no longer be called an 'up and coming startup'. She got pissy at me, but in the end, as usual, I Venmoed her a few bucks so she could at least keep the lights on and watch her reality TV shows.

I vowed to hide the remote from my stepdad the next time I went over, though.

I snuggled back into my seat, wondering how Gabriel found such great tickets. It seemed suspicious, but I decided not to think about it, considering how fantastic the seats were. They were center and a few rows back from the front, just the way I liked it. Too close to the front and you had to crane your neck the whole time, and the last thing I needed was more neck cramps while I was trying to study. This must be a treat for him, too. Bakers didn't make that much money. I knew that from Stepdad #3. I was already worried about the blanket he gave me. Probably set him back a week of salary, and I didn't want such a nice guy to feel like he had to do that for me. I'd have to make it up to him somehow. Just had to figure out how.

I tried hard to concentrate on the play and just about succeeded. Too bad there was a better show to my left. It was clear by Gabriel's expressions that he was enjoying the show, and that made me fill with warm, fuzzy feelings. I kept sneaking glances over, watching his handsome face light up with excitement when Bob Cratchit got hugs from his family, or fill with worry about whether Tiny Tim would make it and get enough to eat. I was close enough to tell his hair was freshly washed and that he preferred citrus and mint body wash. I groaned internally. This evening would be so much easier if he was into Axe body spray.

But that didn't matter anyway. This was a non-date. I needed an addition in my life like a Kardashian needed another dollar.

This was a simple meal to get proper Omega 3 nutrients to my body, then back home to study like the good girl I was.

But at the end, when Scrooge brought over food, and Gabriel's face broke out into happiness, I knew I'd be replaying that vision before I fell asleep that night.

❄

"Are you hungry?" Gabriel asked as we strolled to the escalators to the first level where The Fish Bar was located. Christmas music filled the air, and Christmas lights twinkled in the dark through the windows. This place was truly magical, especially this time of year.

His hand was so close to mine as we walked that I wondered what would happen if I reached over and grabbed it. I clutched my purse strap and tightened my grip around it to quit tempting myself.

"Starving," I answered truthfully. I barely had time to eat all day and only managed to cram down some carrot sticks between customers at work. What I didn't mention was that I was craving a big juicy cheeseburger and not a small pile of fish. I never understood those girls who acted like they didn't eat. I wanted a pile of food, dang it, and I wanted it now. But if The Fish Bar was where Gabriel had a gift card, well, that's where we'd go. Not like I was in the position to be snobby about it. I could barely afford to treat us to Five Guys. Though, right about now, Five Guys sounded amazing. Unlimited fries? Sign me up.

Gabriel excused himself to the restroom, and I took the opportunity to sit on a bench and scroll through The Fish Bar's menu, wrinkling my nose as I read through it. *Thirty-seven bucks for six scallops in sauce? And that was one of the most reasonable dinners, too. Over sixty bucks for a steak?* Who had money for that type of thing? Well. Gift card or no gift card, I'd never order a sixty-dollar steak on someone else's dime, so I'd have to make do with a few scallops. I just hoped the bread basket came with free refills.

Gabriel emerged from the restroom, looking panicked. "Hey, there's been a bit of an emergency at work. The bakery has about ten orders for tomorrow, and the overnight person called in sick. I need to go in. I'm so sorry."

My shoulders involuntarily drooped, but I was already standing up. "No worries," I assured him, the words choking out around the ball of ice that seemed to grow in my throat. It was just the nature of his job, I guessed. But my stomach clenched, and not just because it was empty. The night was going so well. Maybe I could at least swing through Taco Bell on the way home and rescue my evening somewhat. Taco Bell was no substitute for a sexy man, but at least it'd be better than scallops, so it was a partial win.

He eyed me. Feeling me out. "I don't suppose you'd want to come with me, would you? I won't require you to bake, but I could order us some food and we could hang out? Maybe a pizza? From DeLuce's?"

My stomach rumbled before my mouth could speak. DeLuce's was my favorite pizza place in the city.

Gabriel grinned at the sound. "Your stomach seems to agree with the idea. But are you sure you won't miss The Fish Bar?"

"Let's see. On one hand, we can get overpriced crab legs that will still leave me hungry at the end. On the other, twenty bucks will get me my own large pizza and extra dipping sauce. Hmmm..." I tapped my chin as I pretended to think about it.

"Ah, a woman after my own heart. I think. But only if the extra sauce is marinara, not ranch. I don't understand the heathens who put ranch on pizza."

I stopped short at this outrage. "Gabriel, I will not stand for such disrespect in my life. I'll have you know that ranch is the best sauce for pizza. End of story, do not pass go, do not even try to convince me otherwise."

He clasped a hand over his mouth in mock horror. "And here I thought you were the perfect woman. Guess even I can be wrong."

"Oh," I said, quite aware that my voice was taking on a flirtatious tone to match his. Was I okay with that? Did I want him to be flirting with me? The answer to those questions apparently didn't matter because my mouth had a mind of its own. "Well. You can be wrong. But not about me not being the perfect woman. Just wrong about even more important things. Like pizza sauces."

He pulled out his phone and put the other hand over his heart. "I regret my words and can only offer you my heartfelt apologies and promises to become a better man in the future. Can I convince you to forgive me if I order double of both in an act of contrition?"

I crossed my arms as I considered this. One must learn to forgive and forget, no? "Okay, but only if you throw in a Christmas cookie when we get to the bakery. As long as your boss won't mind," I hastily added at the end, all joking aside. The last thing I wanted to do when he was being so nice was to get him in trouble with his boss.

"It'll be fine," he muttered as he tapped at the screen, then held it up triumphantly a few seconds later. "Food will be there in forty-five. Let's head to the bakery and get ready."

I followed Gabriel out to the parking lot and into the icy cold, the wind hitting me like a sharp knife. I blinked in surprise as we rounded the corner. It looked like I wasn't too far off the mark when I imagined being stuck in a murder van.

"Sorry," he apologized as he cleared off the front seat. "I'm stuck with the bakery van right now."

"No worries," I said again. A car didn't make a person, I

reminded myself. Besides, it wasn't like anyone was granting me Sexy Car of the Year ribbons in my old Honda Accord. He probably had a car of his own. Or I at least hoped so.

Gabriel tossed me an apron as soon as we walked through the door. "I don't want you to get that fancy dress of yours dirty. By the way, if I didn't tell you yet, you look stunning in it." He had, in fact, already told me when we sat down in the theater, but my heart thumped hearing it again. I caught the apron. It really would be a shame to get it dirty considering how much it cost. Well, retail cost, that is. I only spent forty bucks on the dress after my discount.

He crossed over to help me tie the ribbon behind my back. His breath swept across the exposed skin of my neck, sending goosebumps down my spine. The scent of his apron, smelling of cinnamon and baked goods, surrounded me and warmed me up like a wool blanket on a cold night. He gathered my hair gently and draped it over my shoulder. My breath caught when his fingers grazed my back as he tied the bow. And, was it my imagination, or did he not know how to tie a bow, because he seemed to take a long time tying it around my neck. I was almost bummed when he finally got the knot just right and stepped away.

I leaned against the counter, taking in the sight in front of me. Gabriel lined up several round cake pans on the island, then deftly started opening up various containers full of sugar, flour, and a variety of other ingredients. I had never seen a military operation for baked goods, but if I were to imagine what one looked like, this would be it.

His gaze caught mine and a sexy smile curled up on his lips. I caught myself smiling back, heart beating faster than was necessary for a moment in a back room of a bakery. "Crazy, eh? Just think, all this work and the cakes will be gone in minutes."

To distract myself from the flush I felt creeping up my

cheeks, I crossed over to help him scoop butter into the massive bowl of an industrial-sized mixer. He handed me a scoop for the sugar, our fingers brushing, and I jolted from the electricity. We spent the next several minutes blending ingredients until a creamy ivory batter was formed.

Gabriel wiped his forehead with his arm. Lifting cakes must be more labor intensive than I realized since his arm was exceptionally muscular. "Pizza should be here soon. Mind if we put this into the pans then they can bake while we eat?"

"Show me the way, partner." We grinned at each other and despite myself, I knew dang well by the flutter in my stomach that I was growing attracted to this baker man.

❄

BY THE TIME eleven rolled around, we had been baking for several hours. Gabriel caught me stretching my arms over my head as I thought about the studying I still had in front of me before I could go to sleep.

"You better get going. It's late, and I can take it from here. I really owe you one for helping me out here. Can I make it up to you?"

I tried to protest that I wasn't tired, but a yawn came out instead. "I don't know, can you fold jeans and hang sweaters?" I joked.

He came close to me, mock resting his head on my shoulder. Fireworks shot off the top of my head into the sky. He smelled like frosting and freshly baked cake. "I do my own laundry, can't be that far off, can it?"

"A man who bakes, loves his grandpa, and does his own laundry?" I started to tease. "Sounds like—"

"Ha!" He removed his head from my shoulder. I never realized how empty it felt until he did so. Till now. "Sounds like the basic life skills every man should know."

That's not exactly where I was going with my joke, but now that he said it out loud, I rather liked it. Maybe I should tell my mother this theory. Speaking of, I glanced down at my phone. Three text messages, asking me what I was doing, then why I wasn't answering her, then one more demanding I call her first thing in the morning. Not too bad for her.

Gabriel caught me looking at my phone, and insisted on calling me an Uber car despite my objections that I'd be fine. "No woman will be walking in the cold, dark night while I'm around," he declared.

"Male chauvinist, huh?" I teased back, though I was secretly impressed. "I studied that in my classes." I thought about telling him my goal to get into the PhD program but stopped myself. If there was one thing I hated, it was talking dreams not actions. And right now, the PhD was still firmly in the dream stage.

Luckily, Gabriel didn't notice my pause as he checked to see where the Uber was. "Ha. I dunno. I'll have to ask Grandpa."

That was a weird comment, but I lost all train of thought as he walked me to the door, pausing before the cold night. "I had a wonderful time with you, Maria."

I panicked as he tilted his body toward mine. Was he going to kiss me? *Please*, screamed my brain. And my head. And my mouth.

Sadly, they were all met with disappointment when all he did was envelop me in a hug, even if it was the most warming hug of my life. One that wanted me to bottle up the essence and sell it at Nordstrom and make a fortune in the winter because, when he wrapped his arms around me, every night chill ceased to exist.

He pulled back for a second, and I thought I was being given a second chance in life. Was this it? He seemed to hesitate a second. *Kiss me now*, my mouth demanded, but unfortunately, his lips didn't get the memo, because all they did was say, "The Uber is here."

Oh. Okay. I guessed that worked too.

Two hours later, after I read three chapters in my textbook and brushed my teeth, I climbed into bed with my new blanket weighing me down. For the first time in weeks, I slept like a rock, with Gabriel's sexy smile the last thing on my mind before I drifted off to sleep.

8

GABRIEL

"So what's with the good mood?" Grandpa leaned against the bakery counter, narrowly missing the garland Mykenna had artistically draped across the front. "Whistling usually isn't your thing."

"And neither is you coming in here to get your baked goods. I'm usually a one-man DoorDash for you," I shot back.

Grandpa grinned. "What can I say? I was thirsty this morning. And that fancy expensive car of yours is still in the shop."

"Yep. Said it'll be another week, too. I guess that's what I get for buying a foreign car." My needs were simple, and I wasn't much on spending all the money I earned from this bakery, but Audis were a weak spot for me, ever since I spent a couple of years in Europe.

He crossed over behind the counter and helped himself to a cup of coffee. I narrowed my eyes, noticing he took my favorite Christmas mug, the one that said "Santa is my Homie" in obnoxious red letters.

He took a sip, meeting my eyes. I wondered if this was some establishing dominance thing, some kind of tactic he used on his patients to get them to spill. You never knew what was going on in that crafty mind of Grandpa's.

"You establishing dominance over there or something?"

"Establishing dominance? Of course not. What a silly thing to ask. It was the only clean mug over there, and I didn't want to use a paper cup and put unnecessary waste into the planet."

Uh-huh. Sure, Grandpa. I started arranging what was left of the day's baked goods while I had a quiet moment. Two trays left. Not bad for a snowy, cold Friday afternoon. I'd definitely sell out by closing time.

"Hey, can you bag up one of those monkey breads for June? She's sweet on them."

"And you're sweet on her." My eyes cut over to him as I bagged up the pastry. I threw in a couple of croissants for her, too. They'd freeze well for later.

Grandpa took another sip of his coffee, feigning innocence. "Me? I'm too old for that nonsense. I know who's not, though. She like the blanket you got her?"

True to Grandpa's promise, he texted me over and over again the day after my date-slash-non-date. I had been able to give him the bare minimum but spent most of Sunday trying to catch up on the cake orders. Having a person out during my busiest season of the year was no joke. If Mykenna didn't get better, I'd have to hire some temporary help. Can't be charging seventy bucks a pop for fancy French Christmas cakes shaped like logs or Santa hats and have them coming out tasting like crap because I was so rushed I mistook salt for sugar or something. I'd ruin my reputation and put all those fancy awards I won out to dust.

"If you're insisting on hanging out, at least come back here and give me a hand." I gestured to a pile of white boxes. Next to them was a pile of custom red stickers with the bakery's logo. I'd splurged to get a designer to create a Christmas-themed sticker for the boxes this season, and now the words Spruce Pâtisserie flowed across the top of the stickers in fancy gold lettering. The red reminded me of Maria's lipstick, which reminded me of her glossy black hair…My mind drifted off for a second, remembering our almost kiss in this very room, by the doorway. I had wanted, with every fiber of my being, to kiss her right before the Uber came, but didn't want to go too far in case she slapped me, or even worse, felt disrespected on a 'non-date'. heck, dating was hard enough but add in non-date elements? A man had to be a mind reader to know what to do.

Grandpa, who put down his coffee cup to fold boxes, interrupted my thoughts. "By the faraway look on your face, it went well, I take it? Me 'forgetting' my paperwork was worth it?"

I started slapping stickers on the boxes and stacking them up, where later today I'd be sliding in cakes and handing them off to my delivery person. "Says who? By the way, that was the least slick thing I've ever seen outside of sandpaper."

"Says your humming 'Friday I'm In Love' by a rock band who came out with the song while you were still in diapers."

"The Cure will *never* be out of style, Grandpa. Ever. Remember that when you're watching *Idol* this season." I looked out at the doom and gloom day. Gray clouds covered the sky, promising snow and no sun was in our immediate future. Just about right for a December day in Minneapolis. The only thing I had to look forward to was a tentative second date with Maria this weekend, though true to her feisty self, she refused to call it a date, instead of calling it a 'get together'. I managed to 'get together' with her once more this week while I helped out Jorge, my driver, who was bogged down with other deliveries; I surprised her with a burrito bowl for lunch between classes. She hugged me so tight after the drop off, I was ready to buy stock in Chipotle.

"So you seeing her again soon?"

"Maybe this weekend," I admitted, slapping on the last sticker. Thirty cakes for delivery tomorrow. If orders kept up like the way they had been, I'd have to seriously think about adding a permanent second van to our rotation. Good thing I had been saving up *Small Town Murder* podcasts all month for this. I'd need the hours of entertainment to get through all the baking. "I made it a casual 'let's see what's up Saturday' comment, so she didn't get spooked."

"That's tomorrow night! June and I are free."

I shot him a glance. "Quit meddling or you'll scare her off. And when are you going to admit to me, and more importantly, yourself, that you totally want June?"

"Want June?" he echoed. "Is that some newfangled terminology? June and I are just friends. Yes, I want to be friends with her."

"Whatever, Gramps." I gave him a bit of stare down and to my surprise, he blushed. Was I right? Was Grandpa actually interested in June? I mean, I had been mostly joking, but now that I peered closer, he *was* suddenly quite interested in the boxes in front of him...Well. That would be amazing if Grandpa found someone after all these years.

As long as he didn't give me *any* details about his love life. As far as I was concerned, no matter any of the crazy stories I heard about East Village, all Grandpa and June did in bed was sleep with long johns on and, I don't know, maybe knit? Read a good mystery novel? Then turned off the lights by 9 p.m. in their own individual beds. That was my image, and I was going to stick with it.

"When are you going to call the lady?" he interrupted my thoughts by grabbing the bag of baked goods for June.

"Right about...now. I'll see you later, okay?"

I was already dialing the phone to Maria.

"Hey, I had a great time with you last night," I started out. "But I'm sorry our date wasn't what I planned."

"Date? I don't date, remember?" But at least Maria's voice wasn't suspicious like it was last time.

I smacked my hand against my forehead even though she couldn't see me. "That's right. My sincere, utmost apologies." I lowered my voice conspiratorially. "You know though, if *you* planned it, it's not a date."

"How do you figure?" Her voice was doubtful but at least I had her listening.

I winged it. "Because. Then it's just...planning. You're making your daily plans, and I happen to be there."

"Oh yeah?" At least she seemed amused at my bluffing. That was a plus. "Anything?"

"Of course," I assured her, though I hoped she didn't plan something crazy like winter skydiving. A man had his limits, after all, and freezing my balls off in the name of love might be just beyond them. Or, even worse, a viewing of any Adam Sandler movies past the year 2000. If it came down to a choice between the two options, I'd have to bundle up and take the jump.

"Well then. I do need to do a little research for my project proposal for Simon...I *guess* you could come along...bump into me and all."

Heck yeah, I cheered internally. I had a second date with this beauty queen. Energy that I didn't have a mere five seconds ago filled my chest, and I had to stop myself from doing a little two-step. Instead of dreading the hours of work ahead of me, I felt like baking cakes for every person on the planet. But, better keep that enthusiasm to myself. Can't scare her off and all.

Out loud, I said, "That makes sense. I did promise to help you after all, and we got sidetracked on Sunday, so I owe you. If it works, I might be outside your apartment Saturday. You know.

In case you wanted to save on carbon emissions and ride together."

"Considering you drive a white van, idling outside my apartment door sounds a bit serial killer-y, wouldn't you say?"

I considered this for a moment. "Serial killing is way too much work for me. I think I'd tap out at one, after seeing all the work it takes to hide a body and all. But I see your point. Uber?"

She laughed, and I pictured her smoldering brown eyes lighting up, which in turn made me light up. "I have to work, anyway. Pick me up at the mall and we'll go from there?"

"It's on." I did a little silent happy dance.

"Oh, and Gabriel? This is *not* a date. I don't date, remember?" Her words were serious, but her tone held a hint of laughter.

"Promise." I clicked off the phone, already wondering what I could bring her this Saturday.

9

MARIA

"A...what?" Luci placed a white paper cup full of liquid heaven on the cash wrap, resting it on a pile of study notes I was using between customers. My arm shot out for the coffee, narrowly missing the pile of snowflake earrings I still hadn't hung up on the miniature Christmas tree display yet.

"A non-date. You know. It's like a date, but not actually one." I took a grateful swig, the hazelnut latte with marshmallow syrup almost burning the roof of my mouth. Today had been yet another day in retail heck, and I was desperate for anything that would distract me from the throngs of shoppers and mountains of Christmas wrapping I had to do. As usual, I was torn between being pissed off that the owner was too cheap to hire a second worker and thankful that I got all the sales goal bonuses to myself. Every shift I spent hours helping people and cramming five-minute study sessions in between customers.

"I kinda gathered that," she answered, walking over to the clearance rack. She held up a black cashmere sweater dress against her. "But to me, it sounds like a regular date that you won't admit is a date." She tilted her head and gave me a knowing look.

I ignored it. "Oh, give me that." I reached my hand out to snatch it from her. "How haven't I seen this?" I flipped the price tag and winced. Even with my generous store discount, it'd cost me almost fifty bucks. Fifty extra bucks that I didn't really have. But it would look great on me tonight for my non-date with Gabriel...

Luci eyed me. "Told you it was a date. If it were you and me hanging out, you'd wear your leggings and hoodie."

"Whatever." I glanced around, and seeing that I had a momentary relief from customers, dashed to the fitting room to try the sweater on. Luci perched against the pink velvet chair to watch my mad dash. I opened the curtain for her approval.

She gave a slight clap. "Put on some tights and booties and you'll be lookin' sexy for...Where is it that you're bringing him on this non-date date thingy?"

I grabbed a belt off the table to cinch my waistline a little more, then paused to consider. With a long gold chain necklace, this would look great... "Purse bingo."

Luci's eyes bugged out and her mouth gaped open like her brain was short-circuiting or something. "What, what the heck did you just say? Your romantic date with a sexy baker with a jawline that could chisel stone is to something called *purse bingo*? Maria, what the heck. You can't take this scenario, which is right out of a cheesy Hallmark movie by the way, with a hot baker and broke single woman, and ruin it all by playing bingo. Bring him to... I don't know... a cooking class where you can oh-so-casually reach around him to stir the pot of boiling soup, and he can show you how to chop an onion by leaning in close, and putting his arms around you from behind as he puts his hand over yours and guides the knife..." Luci's eyes gleamed with excitement at the idea of her favorite Christmas troupe playing out in real life.

I wiggled my eyebrows at her. "And is that how Alex cooks you dinner every night, right before you rip each other's clothes off and have passionate, wild sexytimes on the kitchen floor? Huh. If that's the case, a boyfriend sounds better than I thought."

She deflated a bit. I *knew* it. Neither one of them could cook. "Yeah. I wish. More like we argue over who has to defrost the Trader Joe's meal that night."

"This is a non-date," I reminded her, ripping the tags off the sweater. "And how do you know what he looks like?" Despite her threats to drop by wherever I was going, I refused to double-date with her and Alex, because that would be too date-like.

"I dug around until I found his sister's Instagram. Duh." She rolled her eyes.

I pointedly ignored her and her creeping ways as I thought about our non-date tonight. I plotted for ages, trying to figure out the most non-romantic place to bring Gabriel. Sculpture garden? Cross that off the list, it might actually be fun. World's largest ball of twine? Tempting. I would definitely keep that in mind. I lingered at the SPAM Museum's website. *Ooh*, that would be perfect. There was nothing romantic about disgusting canned meat. Too bad it was over an hour's drive away. Regretfully, I moved on. A few minutes later, after some intense googling on events in the city, I hit upon the best thing. Purse bingo. No way could any red-blooded man consider a trip up to the northern suburbs--to play bingo with crowds of women drinking boxed wine while dreaming of winning a Coach handbag--romantic. I had rubbed my hands with glee when I found the event and quickly secured two spots.

And, it came with a bonus. "No. We're doing bingo because I

can use it for research for the East Village Outreach program. Fundraising events or something."

"Then why'd you get a fresh mani?" she said, her eyes telling me I wasn't fooling her.

❄

Gabriel pulled up in his work van exactly on time. I paused before jumping in. Did Gabriel even *own* a car of his own? Or did he just drive a white bakery van around to save on gas and insurance and let the bakery take on that expense? I tried to squash the thought down—along with the memories of how Ricky, my current stepdad, liked to brag about milking 'the man' for everything he could get—and opened the door. Sitting on the front seat was a beautiful dried floral arrangement, tied up in a burlap ribbon.

"Wow," I gasped, placing it on my lap so my butt didn't smoosh the flowers. "Those are gorgeous. What lucky customer gets *those* on her cake? Is it a wedding cake? Some bride pretending her snowy winter wedding is really a summer beach wedding? Giving it the old 'if you dream it, it will come' shot?" I gingerly placed the flowers in my lap, stroking a petal. I *loved* flowers but never bought them. Who could spend money on something only to watch it die? Not me with my paycheck.

Gabriel started pulling the big van out of the lot after I typed the address in my phone, carefully waiting for a smaller Hyundai to take the curve. "You need to brush up on your '80s movies. The line is *clearly* 'if you build it, he will come'."

I cut my eyes over to him. Was he right? I frantically tried to remember. "And how would *you* know? Isn't that movie before your time?"

He tsk-tsked. "Young Maria, you have so much to learn. First, barely before my time. And yours, might I add. Second, *everyone* knows that the '80s and '90s were the epitome era of great movies. And life."

"Not true." My voice held firm, and I quickly glanced at my phone to make sure we were going the right way. "Name me *one* thing that was better in the '90s than the following decades. I'll sit here and wait. Won't be holding my breath, though."

"Answering machines," he replied immediately. "You used to be able to go all day and pretend you didn't get someone's message. Now? You have to act like you're dead to avoid their call, voicemail, and text messages."

"Fine," I grumbled. He got me there. Only one thing was worse than getting a call from an unrecognized number and not having enough time to Google it before deciding to answer it or not. My mother calling around the end of the month when rent was due. "*Nothing* else, though."

"Siri said 35W South, right?"

I nodded.

"And you're definitely wrong. I can make a big list of things that were better back then. Starting with fashion."

I snapped back into the seat and my eyes narrowed even though he couldn't see me. He was *so* dead wrong. "*No.* Do *not* tell me that you liked baggy jeans back in high school. I will get out of the van right now to save my dignity. Now for the women? Low rise jeans were the freshest thing ever. At least to my high school metabolism. Nowadays, my waistline and carb habit cry in relief that high waisted leggings are in style."

"You know," he gave an impish side-eye, the one I had seen the first night we met and immediately seared into my corneas. He didn't take his eyes off the icy road, which I appreciated. "My high school girlfriend had the sexiest outfit. It was this pink zebra print skirt, and she wore it with a bright pink puffy sleeve shirt and a black hat. It was hot as heck to my sixteen-year-old self, especially when she wore it with her black ankle boots."

"I see that she, too, fell victim to the fashion statements of Hannah Montana," I mused. Even as I said it, hot jealousy flashed through me at this woman from over a decade ago. I decided I needed to distract myself before I went on an ill-advised Instagram scavenger hunt for her. "Bet you were sad that the whole Britney and Justin denim era was a little too forgone for you guys. Would have made a great prom pic for your Gramps to display on his TV stand."

We pulled up to a nondescript brick building before he could retort back. "Hey, where are we? Do our plans involve trying to outrun ghosts in an abandoned warehouse? Because I have to warn you, I ran track in high school, and you won't stand a chance."

I smirked. "But you're a baker these days, so I might have an edge in this modern era." I reached over and patted his belly. *Oof.* I did it as a joke, but I wasn't expecting to find his abs so rock hard. You could bounce a quarter off those things. How did he manage that? By baking all day and working out all night? When did the guy sleep? Did he figure out how to do some ab crunches in his sleep, and if so, could he teach me his secrets? Better yet, give me a quick flash of what was under his shirt, just for science? I put my hand on the car door, my fingers still burning with the memory of touching his abs. I had a feeling my fingertips would be flaming all night.

"It's a surprise." I grinned in anticipation of what he would think when his non-romantic non-date turned out to be the event of most men's nightmares.

Right before we went out into the cold, Gabriel paused. "Oh, Maria? Before we go? The flowers are for you. I wanted to get something that would last."

My mischievous grin melted right off my face as my mouth opened in shock, heart hammering away happily.

10

GABRIEL

I walked into the brick building with narrowed eyes. This building looked suspiciously like a VFW bar, and just the thought of it sent an instant shot of horror shuddering down my spine. The last time I was in one was years ago when I was newly back in the US after my training in France. Trying to catch up with old friends, I had stupidly agreed to an old friend's twenty-first birthday party, which started out calmly enough with dinner. But, in true twenty-one-year-old male fashion, it quickly evolved into multiple rounds of the cheapest shots on special, and somehow ended up with even cheaper beers at the local VFW, then a rousing night of singing karaoke. I woke up the next morning to three new friend requests from females I didn't recognize, a charge for forty-seven dollars to Taco Bell on my credit card, and a desperate need for a breakfast of Advil and Gatorade. I had to admit, my drunken version of "Hotel California" was pretty good that night, at least based on the video floating around on YouTube, but I was reasonably sure Maria wouldn't be impressed with a repeat of that night. And my aging stomach *definitely* no longer had the iron lining that would be required for Act II.

I snuck a quick peek at Maria as she stopped at a woman sitting behind a laminate folding table, holding a piece of paper and highlighter. As usual, Maria looked stunning, with her long glossy black curls pulled up in a high ponytail and makeup done just right. I liked how she didn't cake it on like some women did. I had a feeling she'd look even better without it. I glided my eyes down her body, wondering if her black sweater dress and leggings were considered 'casual cool' like my sister constantly posted about on her fashion account. I flicked through it once a week or so, liking the photos as a good big brother should, but most of the time, everything all looked more or less the same to me. I glanced down at my usual uniform of jeans and a long-sleeved black shirt, wondering what Maria thought of my own outfits. My outfits certainly weren't going to make any fashion spreads, that's for sure, even if I did swap out the long-sleeve for a short-sleeve in the summer.

"Ready for your big night?" She grinned at me like she had a secret. I'd agree to anything to get her to smile like that again. If tonight was another round of Gabriel Sings Crappy Karaoke and I had to do an encore of "Take it to the Limit", so be it. It'd be worth every warbled note. Maria had totally lit up when I told her the flowers were for her, and this one about topped that grin. I filed away those memories in the mental album I created last week called "Maria's Smile." I had already had it on replay several times this week when I needed a boost during the long hours at my bakery.

"Ready," I said, offering her my arm gallantly. She slipped a hand through—score!—and we entered a room full of more women, more folding tables, and...I blinked.

"You brought me to *bingo?*"

Her lips tilted in a triumphant grin. "Not just any bingo. *Purse* bingo."

I stopped in my tracks. "What in the heck is *purse* bingo?"

Instead of answering, she gestured to the front of the room. In my bewilderment at where I was about to spend my Saturday night, I initially missed a table piled high of purses with labels I only recognized from having a mother and three sisters. Coach. Michael Kors. And the grand prize, put on a little stand above the rest, was a..."Tory Burch bags are the prize?"

"Wait, you *know* these brands?" She did a double-take, as surprised as if I told her I knew the cure for the common cold.

"Triplet teenage sisters, remember? Stuff like this tends to come up. Especially when they start hinting about Christmas presents starting in October. It's enough to make a man go broke," I joked. Really though, one thing that was nice about having such a successful bakery was that it allowed me to to spoil my little sisters a bit during the holidays. Made all the long hours worth it. I didn't care so much about buying things for myself, but I loved my sisters like a fierce, overprotective brother bear.

"Shall we go in, see if I can save a few bucks this season by winning them prizes?" I gestured to the man at the fanciest folding table, the one with a black plastic tablecloth covering it. In front of him were various packages, showing us that we could choose from a selection of the local liquor store's best boxed wines this evening. "Grab our seats while I get drinks. Do you prefer gasoline-tasting white or gut rot red?"

She swatted my shoulder. "Boxed wine is the shizznit, I'll have you know. And I'll take a white zinfandel, thanks. I find when it comes to cheap wine, go big or go home is the name of the game."

"Ah, an intelligent lady, I see."

I chuckled all the way to the bartender, where, in an exceptionally good mood, I stuffed a twenty-dollar bill in the tip jar and wished him a Merry Christmas. I checked out the surroundings as he gave me a generous pour in the plastic cups. Of all places that I thought Maria would bring me on a cold winter's night, purse bingo had to be at the bottom of my list. Probably that whole "non-date" kick of hers, trying to find the least romantic place in the Twin Cities. Well, she certainly succeeded. I wouldn't go as far as to call an evening of purse bingo romantic, but at least this was one minor step up from drunken VFW karaoke, so I was still winning.

Too bad she didn't know that, back when I was a kid, Grandma babysat me while my parents worked. Grandma loved bingo, and I had developed quite the deft hand when it came to a dabber.

"I can't believe it," Maria said three hours later, as we scurried into the VFW hallway. "You're insatiable when it comes to bingo. I honestly thought you'd want to play a game or two, then GTFO."

I grinned at her as she leaned up against the wall. Bingo was over, but the socializing wasn't. As soon as the last prize was won, the tables started getting folded up and the karaoke machine set up. One look at that thing and I was done for the evening.

"Had to see it to the bitter end. I wasn't about to let any woman snatch that Tory Burch purse out from behind my back. Not after I had my eye on it all night."

Nestled next to my feet was the coveted bag. It had only taken me twenty bingo cards to get, and honestly, it probably would have been cheaper to buy it outright, but after three determined hours, the bag was *mine*. I yelled out BINGO so loud that we had to make a mad dash out the door as soon as I collected my prize to escape a rioting hoard of purse-hungry women.

"Think you got some good research for the East Village Outreach program?" A strand of Maria's hair came out of her ponytail, and I reached over to tuck it back in. Behind us, the sounds of a man's garbled voice wrapping up "Blue Christmas" turned Elvis Presley over in his grave.

"Mmmhmm. I was thinking something like this, but with some kind of entry fee, which would be used for donations to a cause. Or we'll involve some kids. Something to amp up the stakes." Her voice was a little breathless.

"Yeah?" I traced my finger down the side of her face, wishing that we were anywhere but in a dimmed VFW hallway with scuffed linoleum tiles beneath our feet and extra folding chairs lined up against the wall, listening to people butcher throwback songs from days long gone. At least it was somewhat festive, with a faded cardboard cutout of a Christmas tree leaning against the wall.

"Yeah." She tilted her head back, and I saw the fiery ring around her irises. "Have any other ideas for me?"

The VFW hallway that smelled vaguely like Friday Night Fish Frys of the past be damned. I couldn't take it anymore. I had to touch her. Taste her. "Just one," I answered, then leaned over and brushed my lips against hers to the tune of a forty-year-old woman singing "Don't Go Chasing Waterfalls."

As she kissed me back hungrily, I knew I'd never listen to TLC the same way again.

11

MARIA

Luci stomped through the doors of Bon Marche, knocking the last bit of slush off her boots. "It's negative a million out there," she bellowed. "Why couldn't we Zoom?"

I continued to fold the green miniskirts I displayed next to the red plaid scarves, not even looking at her. "You really need to leave your apartment on occasion."

"Sorry, Ms. Judgeyface, but I have the Internet, a fireplace, and snacks at home. Why do I need to leave it?"

Finishing my stack, I crossed over to start folding up gift boxes. "Because I only have fifty things to do before finals, and I'm trying to multitask. At least here, if a customer comes in, you can pretend you're shopping."

"Fine. But I demand a drink before we start." Luci ran out the door. "Back in ten."

"Why didn't you grab them before you came in?" I shouted after her, but she was already gone.

I shook my head, grateful she was here. I desperately needed help with the project and brainstorming ideas. My first draft to Simon was due December 20th, and finals were two days later, not to mention the holidays after. If I wanted to get everything done in time, major multitasking was in order. I reached for a stack of snowflake-covered socks to hang on the Christmas tree in the corner when my phone dinged, a high-pitched chirp that was my mother's text alert.

Mom: Free for dinner tonight?
Maria: Busy tonight, sorry.

I shoved my phone back into the drawer. I didn't have time for her right now. Dinner was code for Mom was hungry and wanted to eat out, but didn't want to pay. I knew that as much as I knew it would come with a request for something, whether it be cash or help with some scheme or another.

True to her word, Luci was back shortly, with Christmas cookies and steaming cups of hot hazelnut mocha.

"Doppio, right?" I confirmed. One shot would do nothing when I was running on fumes between all my responsibilities.

She rolled her eyes. "I didn't mess around this time. Got you three espresso shots, whatever you call that. Because last time when I got just one, you freaked out so badly that I had to go back for an emergency cup."

I nodded, remembering. She did have to do that, and I stood by my reaction.

Before I could say anything, I was distracted by the FedEx delivery person, with a dolly full of boxes. "Stack them there," I said cheerfully, gesturing to a corner where he could place today's orders.

"I'd like him to stack me," Luci murmured under her breath, low enough so he couldn't hear her.

I gave her shoulder a slight shove. Half a decibel louder and he'd hear us. "What does that even mean?" I hissed back.

"I have no idea, but if you were a smarter woman, you'd have yourself a little "Legally Blonde" moment." We both peeked at him out of the corner of our eyes as we pretended to organize a rack.

Luci wasn't wrong, though. Randall was the only delivery person I'd ever met who could make a FedEx uniform fit like he got it off the floor at Saks. Might have something to do with his incredible body and tight abs.

"Yeah? Think a little 'bend and snap' action still works? And you're confusing your companies. He was a UPS guy in the movie," I hissed under my breath.

Luci opened her mouth to reply when Randall turned toward me, holding out the signature machine. I carefully stepped on her foot as I reached out for it. I'd die if he heard us.

"Bye, Randall! See you next time!"

"See ya later, Paulette!" he called as he walked out the door, his long dreadlocks swaying behind him.

I covered my face with my hands, horrified he heard us. "I can't believe you did that! I'm going to have to quit my job. Move across town. Heck, move across the country," I spoke from behind my fingers.

"Awww, Gabriel will miss you so much." She stuck out her lip and pouted on my behalf.

"And that's just it! I don't even have a crush on this guy because I—" I stopped, realizing I walked right into her trap. I narrowed my eyes. "You set me up to admit I like him," I accused her. Dang it.

She hopped up on the counter and took a sip of her drink. "I knew it!" she crowed. "Alex owes me ten bucks now! He swore you'd never admit you were into him out loud."

"Yeah, well," I grumbled, even as I grudgingly admitted to myself that it was pretty smart of her. And sneaky as heck.

"So how was your—what did you call it? Research? Did you

"research" Gabriel's stunning hazel eyes?" she smirked, passing me my cookie.

"Quit creeping his profile," I barked as I bit the head off of a snowman. "And if you must know, yes."

"I knew it again! Twenty bucks!" She pumped her fist and started tapping on her phone, probably letting Alex know all about her victory. "This will cover the new ornaments I've been eying for our tree."

"Will you and Alex quit betting on my love life?" I cried out, spewing a few crumbs.

She shrugged. "Can't. It's wintertime and we're all coupled up and boring. Need to entertain ourselves somehow."

"Well, glad I could help." I grinned at the memory of our last non-date in spite of myself. "We kissed. And it was amazing. Butterflies flapped, a choir sang, and all that junk."

"Ooooh!" Luci squealed, dropping her phone. "More deets. Stat."

I walked over to the cash wrap and pulled out the Tory Burch bag. "He won this last night. Insisted I have it."

Luci's eyes widened. "It's gorgeous. Keep it forever. And ever. And pass it down to your first granddaughter."

"Yeah, well, you're getting a little ahead of yourself there, missy. First, I need to get through the next two and a half weeks."

Her comment though, made me feel warm and fuzzy. I realized last night, after he told me about his sisters that I tried so hard not to get too close to him I had gone the opposite direction. That I cut myself off from even letting him share more than the basics, and vice versa. But it was *hard* not to. It was obvious he had a wonderful family who cared about him and a kick-ass grandpa. When it came to families, we were playing in different leagues. Make that different sports all together. What was I supposed to do, tell him about my latest dick-for-brains stepdad and how I had to pay my mom's cell phone bill *again*? I'd die of embarrassment first. People with families like his didn't understand people with families like mine, and the last thing I wanted was to hear sympathies. Being vulnerable invited people's well-meaning intentions that ended up dragging me down worse. They always wanted to suggest cutting my mom off financially, but *they* weren't the ones who had to see her go without, or see her put in extra-long shifts at work when she was getting close to retirement age…if she could ever retire, that is.

"When do you see him next?"

"Who says I am?" I challenged her. "We aren't 'dating'."

She stared at me, hands on hips. I stared back, hands on *my* hips.

I broke after five seconds. "Tonight."

"Whoa, three dates in how long? Two weeks? Oooooooo…." she sang. "Sounds like it's time for the DTR talk!"

"No!" My voice squeaked, even as my cheeks started to burn. "We are *just friends*. I have no time for a boyfriend or love."

"Friends my ass," I would have sworn I heard Luci mutter under her breath, but I decided it was best to ignore her.

"Now, I need your help with the program since you know the people at East Village better than I do. Take a look at the proposal here, and tell me what you think, okay? I need to send it to Simon in a week."

I hoped Luci liked it. I removed all the lame things I initially came up with and added more hip, exciting activities, and community outreach. My latest version included dance lessons, tutoring, and once the weather got a lot warmer, glamping. Woven in were fun nights where they could buy tickets to support charities. I liked it, but felt like I was missing something and I couldn't put my finger on what.

She started scanning it. "So far, so good. Those seniors are pretty wild, aren't they?"

I snorted, remembering the stories Gabriel had filled me in

on while we played bingo. Aqua Zumba sounds innocent enough…until I found out they all did it to ogle the hot young instructor.

Luci groaned. "The first year I tried to do the party for them, I thought we could do cakes and punch. Turns out they wanted liquor and blackjack tables."

She stacked the papers in front of her. "Pretty good. Flesh out some of the ideas and you'll be ready. Maybe *Gabrrrrrriel* can help you with some more ideas. Where are you going?"

I picked up the first sheet and started scratching notes in the corner. "Laser tag."

Her brow lifted in amusement. "My bestie, lover of high heels, hater of germs, and fancy dress aficionado agreed to strap on community vests and run around shooting *lasers* at random people? My, my, my. Should I start shopping for my maid of honor dress now?" She jumped forward and clutched my hand. "Satin. Tell me it'll be pink satin. I want to pull off the whole *"Bridesmaids"* look."

"You and your old movies," I shook her off. "First, pulling off the group look wouldn't work. Due to school, work, and everything else, you are my *only* friend because you were so determined to worm your way into my stony heart, so you'd just be standing there in a pink satin dress looking ridiculous. Second, I have no intention of getting married. My mom's done that quite enough times for the both of us, thank you."

My phone *dinged*. Luci lunged for it. So did I. Since she was closer, she won.

She peeked down at the screen and did a little dance. "It's him! It's him! Should I ask Alex if he's free tonight? Double date?"

"Too soon, you freak. Now hand it over." I held out my hand, ignoring the sudden rush of energy I didn't have a minute ago. It had nothing to do with Gabriel, I decided. Just the caffeine kicking in.

"Ooh la la—" Luci stopped short as she glanced at the screen. "Uh. Here you go."

My hand involuntarily rubbed the back of my neck before I grabbed the phone.

Gabriel: Hey, I'm so sorry about this, but can we reschedule? Emergency at the bakery tonight.

I stared at the phone for a few seconds as my stomach went on a roller coaster ride. Why was I disappointed? It was no big deal. It was a casual non-date, after all. I rescheduled with Luci all the time when I got backed up with school. *Heck, this was probably a good thing,* I told myself. I desperately needed to work on the project for Simon and add more details. Not to mention, finals were less than two weeks away at this point, and I hadn't even started creating a study guide. I needed the time more than I needed to run around in a dirty vest shooting lasers at strangers I didn't know. What was I? A middle schooler? *No,* I decided, tossing my hair. This was good. I was getting too caught up in this whole non-dating thing, anyway. The one thing I promised myself when I got into my master's program was I wouldn't get caught up in relationships. I didn't have the mental energy for men, and the ROI between my time and what they brought to the table was never there, at least in my experience or from what I could tell from my mom and the various leeches she called my stepfathers.

The only explanation I could think of was I took a simple kiss too far. *Kisses were just two people touching their lips together*, I told myself. *Don't be over-analyzing that crap.*

Then why did my heart feel like it shrank a size or two?

I looked up at Luci and forced a grin. "No biggie. I'll see him again sometime. And my mom wanted me to meet up, but I told her I couldn't. Guess I'll get to see her now."

"Well, that's good, I guess," Luci offered, her eyes not leaving mine. She knew about all the struggles I had with my mom. She was the only friend I had ever let meet her. "Right?"

"Right," I lied.

12

GABRIEL

I put my head in my hands. This day was already twenty-five hours long, and according to the clock, it wasn't even evening yet. That filthy liar.

I felt like a pile of you-know-what canceling on Maria, but I was thirty orders behind, my delivery driver called in sick again, and I'd have to work till the wee hours to generate enough for tomorrow's cake orders. I'd make it up to her. Somehow. I stuck my foot out and wheeled my flour bin closer to the stainless steel island, not looking forward to the night ahead of me.

My phone vibrated. I glanced at the name on the screen and cursed under my breath. Grandpa. I loved the old man dearly, but I didn't have a minute to spare if I wanted to sleep before it was time to wake up.

"Hey Gramps," I said, sticking my phone between my shoulder and ear and reaching for my measuring bins, wishing I didn't forget to charge my AirPods. "I don't have a lot of time."

"Heading out tonight with that lovely lady of yours?"

I winced, hating to let him down. "Nope. Mykenna has strep, and Jorge called in. It's me against thirty cakes tonight, and I'm losing the battle big time."

"June and I'll be there in half an hour." His tone informed me that it'd be futile to argue with him.

Hope flowed through my chest even as I fought it down. "I can't let you do that. It's poker night, right? Don't you have some chips to lose?"

"Lose?" he scoffed. "Gabriel, I always win."

"Might want to review your math, Gramps. Last time I checked, just because you have more white poker chips at the end instead of green, doesn't mean you won. Quality over quantity and all."

"Yeah, well," he evaded me. "Sometimes you have to redefine success. We'll be there soon. June can't bake worth crap, but we'll get her to fold boxes and set things while I help you with everything else."

The knot in my stomach loosened a bit. Any help would be welcome help right about now. "Love you, Gramps. Even more than *you* love June."

It was worth the tongue lashing I'd get later to hear his indignant gasp before I hung up, grinning.

❄

HOURS LATER, June was tying string around the last box, and I wiped my forehead with the back of my hand.

"Seriously, you two. I couldn't have done it without you." And it was true. They really saved my ass tonight. I did most of the baking, with Grandpa helping me measure and mix. But June had put together an assembly line of boxes, ordered us food, and kept the good vibes going by blasting her favorite music.

Or, at least she tried with the last one. Grandpa only lasted an hour with The Temptations before he grabbed the phone and turned on his favorite playlist. Clay Aiken's *Merry Christmas with Love*, of course. He was very proud that he had over ten thousand likes combined on all his AI playlists that he shared on Spotify.

"How can I thank you both?"

She waved a hand lazily in the air. "No need. When you're retired, this is the type of thing you look forward to doing. Helping others out." Inspiration struck her. "Maybe after the holidays, we could do some bake sessions with kids who need career direction. Add it to that program list that your lady is coming up with."

"June, you're amazing!" I knew Maria wanted some strong, substantial programs to present to Simon. This idea would not only help out deserving kids, but Maria as well. I was already reaching for my phone to give her the idea. Sure, I could wait, flesh it out a bit more, but I wanted to have some kind of contact with Maria. She was all I had been thinking about for the last few hours.

Gabriel: Crisis averted. And now I got a great idea to share for your program.

"Well, Gabriel, I better get June back. It's getting late and I kept her up last night too."

I winced. "TMI, Grandpa."

June gave me a smack on the arm. "We were watching Netflix."

"Whoa, June, Netflix and chill? *Really* TMI," I teased.

"What's that?" Grandpa asked, coming up behind us with their jackets.

"Google it," I said as they shrugged them on. "I can't be responsible for corrupting your innocent ears. My conscience will never recover."

"Did you just text that girl?" June's eyes were sharp.

"Yes..." I answered, wondering where this was going. Wasn't that a good thing?

"*After* you canceled on her tonight?" she demanded.

"Uhhh..." I realized that no matter what I said, the answer would be wrong to her.

I was correct since she started wagging her finger in my face. "In my day, a man called for a date and certainly called to apologize if he canceled. Not sent a text."

Dang it. June was right, even though I was pretty certain they didn't have texts in her day. It was pretty crappy of me to text her to cancel, then not even explain myself. "I'll call her," I promised.

"Tonight," she ordered, with her hand on the door. "And don't forget to invite her to the East Village Christmas Eve brunch."

I saluted her. That June was a spitfire, all five-foot, one hundred pounds of her. When she looked at me with those steely blue eyes, I knew I wouldn't want to mess with her. No wonder Grandpa was enamored, even if he wouldn't admit it. "Yes, ma'am."

Once they were out the door, I grabbed the phone. I hesitated. Was it too late to call? Ten on a Friday night. She should be up, right?

To my relief, she answered on the first ring. "Well, this is original. A real live phone call." I could hear her smile through the phone.

I smiled back even though she couldn't see me. Even though a few seconds earlier, I was dead on my feet, suddenly I wanted nothing more than to see Maria.

"Yeah, I finished early thanks to getting some help. And I got a new idea for your program." I decided to push my luck a little further. "Want to meet for a late night drink and talk about it? Cosma?"

"Cosma?" she yelped. "I've been in my pajamas for an hour. I can't be bothered to make myself look presentable to go somewhere where they serve twenty-dollar martinis."

I forced my mind away from the thoughts popping into it at the mention of Maria in her pajamas. How good she must look in something more casual than the heels and skirts she always wore. Hearing her voice made me want to see her more. Even with Grandpa and June's help, I had a stressful night, and seeing her would make it better. So, I pivoted to Plan B.

"Fine. Takeout and wine? My place?" I had a decent wine rack thanks to the knowledge I acquired during my time spent in Bordeaux.

She paused, and I could tell she was thinking this through. "This isn't some ploy to get some sexy times, is it?"

"No," I promised, even as her words made me realize I wasn't necessarily opposed to the idea. "I am an honorable, respectful man, and if you jump me, I shall remind you of that fact."

I almost heard her smirk. "Fine. But my place because I'm warm and cozy. And I'm in the middle of studying. And only if you pick up some Thai. I want spring rolls."

"Your wish is my command, m'lady." I clicked off, frantic to find somewhere decent that was still open and could make spring rolls. Luckily, I found a place with four stars down the street that still accepted orders for twenty minutes. I punched in my order quickly, and knowing they probably were cursing my name when they wanted to go home on this snowy night, added a twenty-dollar tip. Forty-five minutes later, I pulled the van up to Maria's apartment, a nondescript brick building by the University.

Gabriel: Knocky-Knock, delivery man
Maria: I see the van. I thought I said Thai, not cake? Go back and get me the goods. 😉

I was tempted to make a joke, but thought better of it. Not with a woman like Maria. Instead, I opened one of the styrofoam containers and snapped a quick pic of the food inside.

Gabriel: See this? But maybe I'm one of those fancy bakers that make cakes that look like food. You'll never know unless you let me in.
Maria: I'll take the gamble. Look up.

I looked up and froze. And not because of the icy cold air that promised that I'd want to run directly from my van to her apartment. Maria stood in the doorway but not the perfectly made up Maria I knew. This version had her hair down, and no makeup. Instead of tights and stiletto booties, she wore leggings and a long fuzzy sweater with snowmen on it. I knew most women thought they looked better dressed up, but if she thought the same, she was wrong. She was a thousand times more beautiful with her casual wavy hair and slippers.

I grabbed the food containers and bolted to the door.

Once we were inside her apartment, I handed her the bottle of wine I brought, a cheap Australian Shiraz. I grimaced a little as I passed it over. It was the only one I could procure on such a short notice, a gift from a customer a few months ago. I had stuck it in my office at the bakery and left it there. Luckily, If Maria noticed the cheap label, she mentioned nothing as she poured us a glass. I checked out my surroundings as she did. The place was small, but true to Maria, classy. I grinned when I saw the dry flower bouquet I gave her on a marble side table. She looked busy too, with notebooks, a laptop, and several textbooks strewn across the table. It was obvious she had been there the better part of the night before I came over.

I took a sip and made a face. This stuff was nasty. I started to apologize but she was opening the boxes and scooping things on plates. "Pad Thai?" she asked, holding up the box like I didn't know what was in it.

"Yes, please." We ate in silence for a minute, both apparently starving.

"So, what did you do tonight when I was stuck at the bakery?" I took another sip of the awful wine, hoping that the air helped improve it a bit. Nope. A bottle like this deserved to go straight down the drain.

Maria's eyebrows pinched together for a second, her mouth in a straight line. Then, they smoothed out so fast I wondered if I imagined things. Or if she was seriously pissed off that I canceled on laser tag. Or, even worse, was really into laser tag and mad that she didn't get to play tonight? If that was the situation, I really didn't know how I'd handle it. That was a lie. I knew I'd handle it by signing up for a season's pass and professional laser tag lessons from a pro.

"You okay, Maria?" I took yet another swing of wine. Even if it tasted like rotten grapes, I needed it to calm my nervous mind. Maybe I needed "Tell me a story about you when you were little. Your favorite memory."

Maria hesitated, and I teased her a little. "Got too many? You chasing the boys around the playground? Or were you a naughty child and got coal in your stocking?"

She took a sip of wine. "One time, when I was young, my mom woke me up one morning and told me we were going to a theme park. You know Paul Bunyan Land up north in Brainerd?"

I nodded. "Yep, I've been there. I thought it was the best when he said hi and used my name." It was one of the biggest draws of the theme park, and it took me years to catch on that the massive Paul Bunyan statue only knew my name because Grandpa told one of the workers.

"I loved that too," she laughed, and a wave of relief went

through me at her obvious relaxation. Whatever was bothering her earlier seemed to be gone.

"I got to go on the merry-go-round, Tilt-a-Whirl, and Mom got me cotton candy. I thought it was the most amazing day of my life. Probably because it was."

"I know!" I exclaimed. "It was the best when I was five."

Her face took on that weird look for just a second before smoothing out again, and I brushed a lock of her hair off her shoulder, letting my hand linger. She reached up and intertwined her fingers with mine, sending my heart into a Tilt-a-Whirl of its own. Whatever she thought about a second ago was obviously no longer bothering her.

"That's so adorable," I murmured, my mind imagining us bringing a little Maria or Gabriel of our own there one day.

She gave my fingers a little squeeze. "Want to turn on a movie?"

An opportunity to get closer to her? Only a fool would turn that down. I followed her to the living room, where she flicked on the Christmas classic 'Elf' and looked to me to see if I was okay with it. Even though I had watched it a hundred times, I nodded anyway, and scooched closer, nabbing a throw blanket I found draped over the couch and spreading it across our laps.

And half an hour later, as she put her plate down and reached for my hand, intertwining my fingers with hers once, and pulled herself into my lap, I was glad I didn't need to pay attention to Will Ferrell. Because all my attention was focused on Maria, and the way she kissed me, with her soft lips, slightly floral smell, and the taste of wine. I dug in hungrily, all the exhaustion from the previous hours forgotten. And when she stood up and pulled me off the couch and toward her bedroom, I more than willingly followed.

13
MARIA

I stared at the screen in front of me, the cranberry eggnog muffin in my hand forgotten. My heart came to a stuttering stop and I blinked once, twice, three times. But no matter how much I blinked, the letter didn't change. It was still a C-. Dread settled in my gut and I swallowed down the panic rising in my throat. A C. With a *minus* after it. Just a few small percentage points away from the letter D. The letter bounced through my head like an angry reindeer that didn't get any treats. Like it was the lump of coal in my stocking.

My mind whirled with this newfound information. How did I let this happen? I don't get C's. I earned every dang penny of my scholarship with almost straight A's. Had been that way since I was in middle school. Sure, there was that one time in seventh grade that I got a C, but that was a group project and Ms. Jung said everyone got the same grade, and when Sandra Lindley didn't turn her stuff in, we were all brought down. Ever since then, I had done the work of two people in group projects as insurance. But this? This was my fault. I did it to myself. An ice-cold shiver went down my spine as I realized if I didn't change this grade, my scholarship could be in real jeopardy, and the chances of me getting those letters of recommendations would fly away in the dark night like Rudolph and Dasher and all his other buddies, and I'd be forever stuck just like Mom.

The thought sent an ice-cold shiver of fear down my spine. I couldn't let that happen. Wouldn't. I'd fix this. I just had to figure out what the heck happened.

Gabriel.

His cute dimpled smile floated into my thoughts, and horror struck me with a realization. *I was my mother.* I let a guy steer me off my path. And if I wasn't careful, one that would barrel me right off the road into the icy river, trapping me under metaphorical ice.

"Oh, noooo." I put my head in my hands and shrieked out loud, alarming the man in the round glasses next to me. He looked like he didn't know whether to comfort me or call 911. *Well, buddy, you better call 911 because I got a C- on the most important quiz in Clinical Psychopharmacology.* Though it was a minor assignment overall, every point mattered when I was on a scholarship. Not to mention that it was the basis of the material that would be on the final, clearly showing I wouldn't do well on it in ten very short days.

I was going to have to talk to my professor about it. Argue my way to a better grade. Even as I thought it, I realized my plan was flimsy, but I had no other choice. This was no time to mess around.

Mess around. I winced at those words in my mind, regretting the night when Gabriel showed up with Thai food and that horrible cheap wine, and I slept with him to the bottom of my soul. I had been pissed off when he had canceled on me. I took it as a sign not to get involved and let him go.

But then I went to meet my mom like a good little daughter, even offering to meet her up at a Mexican restaurant, even though I knew it meant I was treating. But, remembering the stipend coming my way for working on the program, I decided it was a charge on my credit card that I wouldn't mind paying off next month. I thought of it as a little pre-Christmas get together. Maybe it'd be fun, having a little mother-daughter dinner over watermelon margaritas. But it ended as usual, with sob stories about how much better my life was than hers, and hints for money, renewing my mindset that I needed to work hard on the Senior Outreach project so I could have a financial cushion when things like that came up.

I ended up in such a downer mood after that I wanted nothing more than to veg out with someone and eat bad food in front of an old movie. Even realizing that he drove the work van yet again, cementing the thought he didn't feel the need to actually get a car of his own, reminding me of a habit of more than one of my mom's boyfriends, didn't deter me that night. Surely a girl deserved a little pick-me-up after such a crappy day, right? Well, looks like I had let him pick me up that night, all right.

"How could you have let it go this far?" I whispered to myself, looking at the grades in front of me. I had the best night with Gabriel earlier this week, and it wasn't because he had the looks of Ryan Reynolds and a rock hard ass that apparently never saw one of the pastries he baked. It was falling asleep next to someone on a cold night. Him brushing a lock of my hair back before leaving at five in the morning to open the bakery, asking me to join him and his grandpa for the Christmas Eve brunch at East Village. My heart had grown ten sizes at the invitation, having something to look forward to instead of just a small get together with my mom and stepdad before joining Luci and Alex at his family's celebration.

But looking at the grade in front of me, it was apparent I let the whole "friends" turned "friends with benefits" thing go too far. I pushed the nagging thought out of my mind. The one I was scared out of my mind about ever since meeting Gabriel. The thought that I was turning into my mother, chasing after good-looking men, and jeopardizing my future in the process. The other night when he asked me to tell him a story about my childhood, I had felt close enough in that moment to open up a bit. But when he assumed I was a little kid when my mom brought me to the theme park, I had mentally clammed up again, too embarrassed to admit I was twelve when the trip happened, long past the typical age for a first trip to a rickety theme park.

Well, Maria, that's the price you pay for having a good time, I thought to myself as I shut the lid of my laptop, ignoring the texts from my mother that popped up on iMessages. She'd just have to wait.

❄

"Uh, Professor Jones? Do you have a minute?" I shrank beneath the steely gaze of my white-haired teacher after class. She might look like Mrs. Claus, but she sure as heck didn't act like it. Of all the classes to struggle with, it had to be *hers.*

"How can I help you, Maria?" Her tone may as well have said, "GTFO of my classroom, Maria, I have a bulgogi bowl waiting for me for lunch and I'll be pissed if it gets cold."

I mustered up my courage. "Can we talk about my quiz grade?" I dug out my phone, flipping through to the screenshot I had taken earlier. "I got a C-."

She barely glanced at the screen. "And?"

I opened my mouth and closed it, trying not to shake. I briefly shut my eyes, just fast enough that she might hopefully confuse it with a blink. This was going to be harder than I thought. Not that I thought it'd be particularly easy in the first place.

"Can you tell me why?" Is what came out instead of what I

planned to say, which was *'based on my essay, I feel I deserved at least a B, blah blah blah.'*

She unplugged her laptop and stuck it in an ancient black tote bag. "Probably because your work has been slipping lately."

A bout of nausea rolled through me as a bead of sweat formed on my temple. "But why?" I blurted out before I could stop myself. As if she'd know. What did I expect? That she was following me around all day, every day? Reading my mind? Then again, she *was* a psychology professor, so if she was worth her paycheck, she should probably have some kind of clue.

She shrugged. "Not sure. Have you been distracted lately? Anything at home bothering you?"

I bowed my head toward my feet, giving her my answer. Her expression softened for a second, which shocked me. Must be the Christmas spirit getting to her, though I always pegged her as more of a Grinch. Pre-epiphany.

"I assume you need a good grade for your portfolio?" Her question caught me off guard, and I nodded mutely, not trusting in my voice.

Trusting myself got me into this position. Trusting that I could balance everything, do it all. How very wrong of me I was. With a sinking feeling, I knew this scene. It was like an old, familiar movie that you didn't particularly enjoy, but it was always somehow on the TV, anyway. I may as well have called it The Story of My Mother.

Every time my mother seemed to get one step ahead in life, she had fallen head over heels with yet another man, and next thing you knew, she'd be putting him first, and herself—and by default, me—last. She would be giddy and happy, and we'd dance around the kitchen in glee, at least for the first few months. Then, like clockwork, after the honeymoon phase ended, reality would hit and her current boyfriend or husband would show his true colors. Rent would start to be late, Mom would need to work overtime to keep up with the bills, and soon enough we'd be handed an eviction notice and made to move in the middle of the night. Same story, different book, time after time. The one thing I vowed when I graduated high school and moved out was that I would never, *ever* let a man bring me down like that. That I would work hard, get a good job, and not depend on anyone. Instead, with one little Christmas cheer, I got caught up with a Gabriel. I wasn't shallow enough to think that a man's profession defined his worth, but I worked too hard toward my goal to let anyone drag me down. I had spent too many years running away from a lifestyle that didn't suit me that I couldn't toss it away with someone I barely knew.

Professor Jones headed to the door which was my cue to follow her. "Tell you what. If you retake it, I'll accept the higher of the two grades. I don't do this often, but you've been a talented student of mine over the years, and we all struggle sometimes." She turned to go right, and even though I needed to go that direction, too, I'd rather die than walk down the long corridor with her, so instead I turned to go left. I'd just have to take the long way around.

"Thank you, Professor Jones. You don't know how much this means to me."

She nodded crisply. "Show me by getting a good grade on the final in two weeks."

I nodded back and fled.

❄

THIS TIME, it was me who showed up at Luci's work. "Hey," I said as I saw her come out the office door.

Luci shrieked loud enough where the security guard turned to look at us, hand on his radio.

"We're okay," I called out, waving him off from calling the cops on me.

"What are you doing here? And why are you sitting in the dark? Ooo! Is it an impromptu happy hour?" Luci's face lit up like the Christmas trees decorating the streets in front of us.

"First, in case you haven't noticed, we live in Minnesota, where it gets dark at approximately early o'clock in the winter. Second, not unless we're drinking 5-Hour Energy drinks, which would make the lamest happy hour ever, no."

Her face fell a bit. "Are vodka and Red Bulls still a thing at least?"

"I love how you didn't even ask why or what we were doing. And no, I don't think they are. Unless you're a frat boy, that is."

We started walking through the skyways to the apartment in the building she shared with Alex.

"I can already guess why the ambush. Study time? East Village Outreach project time?"

I nodded glumly. "Both. All the above. Check the boxes because I got crap to do." I filled her in on the conversation with Professor Jones.

She reached over to rub my back. Well, we'll help. I'll get Alex to order us dinner while I help you with the project. Then afterward, he can help you study. Quiz you and stuff." She was already whipping out her phone to text him.

"Don't want to help me study?" I stuck out my lip in a fake pout, but internally I was forever grateful to her. I never had much time for friends, and always lived the life of a lone wolf, but the day Luci stormed my store was a defining moment in my life. The "before" which was me, doing life on my own, and the "after" which was having someone in my life who cheered me on and championed me.

"No offense, but heck no. Alex can do it. He's a professional.

He can keep you on track, and whip out that teacher voice and everything."

I laughed at the image. Alex taught fifth-grade. Despite the obvious difference in subjects, he probably was better suited to help me out than Luci, who was a software developer.

"Thanks, Luce. I appreciate it."

"Honey, you helped us get together in the first place. We owe you." That was true. Luci and Alex had come into my store separately multiple times, and I had put two and two together, and figured out they were best friends who were madly in love with each other, but didn't know. I had pointed it out to Alex, and the rest had been history.

Her eyes lifted from her phone and cut over to me. "Speaking of..."

I shook my head firmly. "No. I can't get caught up like I have been. I need to take a step back and concentrate on school right now."

"Okay." Luci's left eyebrow rose. "And you told him this?"

I was already shaking my head again. "No need. We're not dating, right? All we ever did were non-dates." I swallowed the lump in my throat that developed after choking out those words.

"You really believe that?" Luci held open the skyway door for me and I crossed through it. I didn't answer her. Because to be honest, I wasn't sure what I believed anymore.

14

GABRIEL

I whistled as I worked, like that old Disney song. I stopped for a second, trying to remember what film it was from. I thought maybe Snow White, but I wasn't quite sure. I shrugged and resumed my dish cleaning. Highly unlikely that Snow White whistled "All I Want for Christmas is You" anyway.

Mom already texted me three times asking for my Christmas list, and I had no idea what to tell her. I was a pretty minimalist person. Give me my bakery, a good Netflix queue, and a nice glass of wine after a hard day's work, and I was a happy man. Or so I thought, up until over two weeks ago. Now I knew all that was fluff. There was one thing I wanted for Christmas, one thing Mom couldn't put under the Christmas tree.

Just the thought of my night with Maria made a grin explode across my face. There was something about Maria that made the days feel brighter. Warmer, too, which was pretty dang hard to do when the temperature averaged under ten degrees and every other weather report seemed to promise more snow. December used to be my least favorite month, with terrible weather coupled with all work and very little play, but somehow that turned around this year. July with the beaches and sunny skies be damned, December is where it was at this year.

I switched from whistling Mariah Carey to Ariana Grande. That one was harder to whistle, so I ended up humming it to myself, giving a little two-step while I was at it.

"Uh, boss, you okay over there?"

I glanced over at Mykenna, my high school aged cashier who was staring at me like I had two heads.

"When you're in a great mood, sometimes you gotta dance, you know?" I explained to her blank face. Mykenna was only ten years or so younger than me, but by the expression on her face, I may as well have been telling her that I was filling out my AARP card application.

"Okay. Just wanted to, like, make sure you weren't having a stroke or something." She went back to the front where she grabbed a spray bottle to wipe down the tables.

"The average age for a stroke is over sixty-five—" I started to call out to her before stopping myself. Apparently, I needed to take the hint. My dancing skills needed a little work. Which gave me an idea...

Gabriel: Know what's a non-date?

I grinned as I typed, remembering her incredible body but even more so, her incredible drive. Maria was still on the not dating kick even after our night at her apartment. I didn't care, she could call it whatever she wanted as long as she was calling me at all. Sure, it drove me a bit crazy that she was a hard cookie to crack, and didn't like to talk much about her schoolwork or the stress I knew she must be under, but I would get there. I'd make it my personal mission.

Maria: What?

I blinked. Not exactly the vibe I hoped for, but I pressed ahead. Maybe I was reading into things too much, I decided. It was a text message, not a voice message.

Gabriel: Free tonight? I saw a meat raffle. That's definitely a non-date, right?

I mean, really, I'd rather get my meat at the grocery store like most people, but I survived purse bingo, so surely I could sit through people raffling off ribeye and pork chops as long as Maria was next to me.

Maria: Sorry, I'm booked tonight.

I saw three dots show up and waited. And waited. They briefly appeared again, then disappeared completely.
I saw three dots show up and waited. And waited. They briefly appeared again, then disappeared completely.
I lingered by my phone another few minutes to see if she would follow it up with our usual banter, but it sat on my desk, where I was working up the weekend orders, silent. I hesitated over it, wondering if I should write back again. I briefly thought of the angry expression the other night that had flashed across her face so briefly that I thought I had imagined it. Maybe I didn't. Maybe I did piss her off? Then why not tell me? She seemed in a better mood later that night. And even better in bed, I thought, grinning at the memory. I've been on the autobahn and had pastries made by the hands of some of the best bakers in Europe. But kissing her was more thrilling than taking an Audi over a hundred and sweeter than the freshest crêpe. A thought struck me then. A thought more horrible than waking up one morning and seeing that a hundred cake orders were placed overnight.

Did Maria think I sucked in bed?

I mean, she seemed to enjoy it, and the quickie I gave her the following morning before I left to open the bakery in the early cold hours. But maybe it wasn't as good for her as it was for me? I had my share of good sex, but sex with her was on another level. It was like all the other times were practice for the real thing, and she was the elixir to show me what real sex was, felt like, and should be.

Finally, I followed it up with a quick message to let me know when she was free, then left her alone like she apparently wanted it, and went back to work, my good mood now completely shot.

※

I WAS STILL CRABBY LATER that night when I dropped off Grandpa's weekly loot.

"What's with you?" he asked as I shoved the bread into his freezer with a little more force than was strictly necessary.

I cursed under my breath. It probably got squished, and I'd have to deliver another loaf later that week if I didn't want him to have flat sandwiches. My special olive oil bread was meant to be light and fluffy, perfect for spreads and meats, not smashed together like a cheap wafer. The thought of Grandpa having flat sandwiches broke my heart for some reason, much worse than it should be, considering I could deliver him a hundred fresh loaves tomorrow if he wanted, and my face fell.

I didn't answer him, and he didn't say a word back. The apartment was silent. Another one of Grandpa's psychology tricks, I knew. Stay silent and the other person felt compelled to start talking.

And unfortunately, it worked on me every time.

"Maria's ignoring me," I burst out.

Grandpa made a little steeple with his hands. "And why do you think that is?"

"I have no idea."

"Hmmmm..." He nodded slowly, looking directly at me.

Dang Grandpa and the tricks up his sleeve. "I mean, I guess she's been overwhelmed at work. And school," I babbled, the words pouring out of me as I tried to create a sense of the situation.

"And how does that make you feel?" his voice was still perfectly neutral.

"Forgotten about," I admitted. "Though I know that's stupid. She insisted all our hang-outs were non-dates. And that she didn't believe in love or relationships." I didn't mention the sex to him. There were some limitations, even if Grandpa was a renowned psychologist who probably heard it all during his career. Sex talk with your grandpa was just wrong, no matter what his profession was. But it was frustrating to me that as much as I tried to get her to open up, ask her about her schoolwork, she would give just a bit then slam shut again like a Venus flytrap, and I didn't know why,

"Ah. A small case of philophobia?"

I walked over to his iPad and searched through Spotify to distract myself. To no one's surprise, all his favored playlists were centered around Carrie Underwood, Kelly Clarkson, and Chris Daughtry. I had no idea what Grandpa just asked me. "I know what phyllo means, does that count?"

He laughed. "Don't worry about it. Just know that this too shall pass. It's a hard season for her. She's probably getting crushed with all her responsibilities."

I brightened at his words, even if they did sound like some wall decal thing. Grandpa was likely correct. I had to give her a little time.

15

MARIA

It was official. I was stressed to the max. I mean, sure I had been stressed out before, studying for the retake. This was nothing new for a graduate student. But adding in a new project, working mad hours, a mom who never quit trying to call me for favors, and studying pushed me to the limit. I had enjoyed my time with Gabriel, but even that proved to be too much for me.

My mind switched to him again. Gabriel was so *nice*. Funny. Had a wonderful grandfather and parents who cared for him. I loved watching him scroll through his pictures, showing me pictures of his triplet sisters and sharing funny stories about them. It was obvious that even though they lived hours away, they were a close-knit family. I had let myself imagine for a brief time what it would be like to have a family like that. Even after he shared about his family, I didn't let on about my mooching mother and rotating stepdads. The thought was too embarrassing. I preferred to keep things light, and hear about him and his family because I certainly didn't have much to say about mine and there was only so much I could talk about Bon Marche.

But allowing myself to live in that fantasy world, even

secondhand, had caused me to stretch myself too thin. Try to be someone that I couldn't be, at least right now. That was even more apparent when my phone started vibrating. My heart leaped for a second, hoping it was Gabriel, but I immediately squashed that. I blew him off. What did I expect, that he'd come over with a bouquet of flowers? My eyes quickly shifted to the dried bouquet he had given me a week ago. I snagged a spare display vase from work, with my boss's permission, of course, and displayed them on the glossy marble coffee table I scored for thirty bucks off Craigslist. The effect was gorgeous and brightened my spirits every time I paced my small apartment, which was quite often these days. Sometimes I wished I had put up some lights or a little tree, but it didn't seem worth the time or expense.

No, of course the call wasn't from Gabriel. It was from my mother, *again*. I slid her an extra hundred for her water bill last week at dinner, so I wasn't sure why she was calling already. With a shot of dread, I picked it up.

"Hi, honey," Mom's voice flowed through the speaker. I shuddered, already knowing where this was going. Mom never called me pet names unless she wanted something. "Just wondering what you were getting Ricky for Christmas."

I clicked on the speakerphone and got up to grab my notes for the East Village Outreach. I had one more week to amp it up and turn it into Simon, and it seemed lacking in some way. May as well go over notes as she drowned on.

"I thought I got him a water bill?" I asked.

"Tee hee." Mom laughed, pretending like I was joking. We both knew I wasn't.

I mean, I had nothing against Ricky, *specifically*. On the surface, he was a good guy. And he treated her well, which was much more than Stepdad #1 and Stepdad #3 could say. No, Ricky, who held the dubious honor of being Stepdad #4, was a perfectly pleasant, gregarious person. It was his hobbies of avoiding paying work, drinking too many martinis, and always chasing the next big money-making scheme or startup that drove me crazy. Mom inevitably ended up putting in more hours than she should at her age, and getting fired because they always had to take off time to go to some rally, like how they could be millionaires if they paid some guy a thousand bucks to teach them how to flip houses. Or, even worse, he'd have a bout of success, a fluke, and bring in a few bucks. He'd get Mom excited, telling her this was *it,* what they had been working for came true, and grandly tell her she should quit her job. Then, like clockwork, the money would disappear in a flurry of bad financial decisions and they'd be broke all over again.

No, this was certainly not a pattern I could tell Gabriel, with the nuclear family and three charming blonde sisters. He already told me about their plans to go on a sleigh ride on Christmas. A frickin' *sleigh ride.* The closest thing I had to a sleigh ride growing up was when Mom borrowed my sleigh to move us in the middle of the night when I was eight.

Gabriel hinted that I should join them, but it was definitely too early to meet his family so I had quickly changed the subject. Going to the East Village Christmas brunch was one thing, considering I already met his grandpa, but going to Christmas Day celebrations with my new friends-with-benefits or whatever we were? Way too awkward. Even worse if he wanted to be invited to mine.

"Well, Ricky really needs a new suit. I was thinking we could go in on one for Christmas? He has that leadership summit coming up next month." Leadership summit, my ass. More like some conference he would pay to go to be told by women wearing massive diamonds that he, too, could afford such things if only he put every single dollar and minute into bothering his friends to buy useless junk they don't need from him.

For Mom, 'going in' was code for 'pay for it and I'll tell you I'll pay you back and never actually do it'. I sighed and abandoned the project plan and instead grabbed my laptop to check my quiz grade. I had retaken it this morning and was waiting for Professor Jones to update my grade in the system.

"I'll give him a gift card to Target. I saw some nice suits there last time I was shopping." At least if I got a gift card, he couldn't use it for something else.

"Target, honey? I was thinking something a little higher quality."

I stared at the screen in horror, no longer hearing her words. Professor Jones uploaded the grade for my retake she let me have, alright. And sure, I had done better, but a C was only marginally better than a C-. I put my head down on the table as tears started to form.

"Target, Mom," I said as my head laid on the table. At least she could use the gift card for groceries if things got tight. "I got to go." I hung up the phone without waiting for an answer and sat there for a few minutes, trying to process everything.

A C in the class I needed the most. A project due in a week. Work that was the busiest of the year. It was clear. I had to prioritize things better than I had been doing. As I made a mental list of everything I had been spending time on over the last few weeks, it was clear there was only one thing I could cut. The one thing I tried to hang on by a thread.

My time with Gabriel.

16

GABRIEL

The bakery had been packed all morning, and it wasn't until two in the afternoon that I could collapse in my office for a much-needed break. I was just thanking Younger Gabriel for having the foresight and intelligence to buy a reclining office chair when Mykenna poked her head into the office.

"Uh, boss?" I had no idea why Mykenna kept insisting on calling me that, but I nodded anyway. "What's up?" Hopefully not much, because all I wanted to do was shut my eyes for a second. Make that nine hundred seconds, the exact number of seconds in fifteen minutes.

"Someone named Simon is on the phone for you?" Her voice went up into a question at the end, and I mentally made a note to coach her on how to be more assertive in the workplace. Later.

Simon? The only Simon I could think of was the director at East Village. But why would he be calling me? With a groan, I pushed myself out of my chair.

"Why don't you take twenty, Mykenna?" Her face looked as exhausted as I felt, and I gave her an envious glance as I watched her collapse into the chair. Poor girl. She had been working her ass off on her winter break from school, and I'd have to put a nice bonus in her paycheck for the holidays. I had slowly grown the patisserie in order to avoid business debt, but in the last year, popularity had taken off to a new level, and I needed to think seriously about scaling up the number of employees because this was unsustainable.

I went to our work phone that Mykenna had left next to a stack of chocolate Santas and picked it up. "Hi Simon, what can I help you with?"

"Hi Gabriel, feel free to say no to this," he started out, and I mentally suppressed a sigh. It wasn't that I didn't like Simon, in fact, I thought he was a great guy. But everyone knew that when a conversation started out that way, a big favor was about to be asked. And I wasn't wrong.

Turns out the caterer for East Village's brunch backed out on them, and they were on a time crunch to find someone. A volunteer ran the party, but since the timing was short, Simon told her he would call around as well.

"So, I don't suppose you do any food, do you? Or is it only bakery items?"

I hesitated. Obviously, my expertise was in French pastries, but I did train at a culinary school for two years, and the bakery offered some light meals. I had the basics down, and Google could help me fill in the rest. I guess I would be able to throw something together in a pinch, but of all weeks to ask, this would be the absolute worst.

"When is the party again?" I asked, stalling for time. Like I didn't know. Like I wasn't invited by Grandpa already. As welcoming and feisty as East Village was, the holidays would always be a lonely time for seniors, with memories of families gone forever, or located too far away to visit. The brunch was one of the anticipated events of the year.

Simon sensed my reluctance. "Don't worry. If I'm asking too much, I'm sure I can get some decent stuff at Costco. My budget is pretty low anyway, to be honest."

That did it. I pictured all the seniors coming into the room for the party, eating cheap sandwich wraps out of plastic trays, and my heart sank. No way could I let them do that when I had the ability to create something a thousand times better. I'd just have to find a twenty-fifth hour in the day to do it all. Maybe Mykenna had a friend or two who wanted to earn a few extra bucks while school was out.

"Do they like roast turkey with chestnuts? Buche de Noel?" I asked, rubbing my forehead. "And don't worry, the food will be *gratis*."

※

I SPENT the rest of the day coming up with a menu that I thought would do the trick between many different dietary needs and my own culinary abilities. Finally, after I made myself a quick sandwich, I was rested enough to tackle the hardest part of my day. Contacting Maria. I winced, thinking about how I was going to have to cancel on bringing her to the brunch, being that I now *was* the brunch. The last thing I wanted to think about was putting disappointment in those chocolate brown eyes. After our latest interactions, I was already worried when I sensed something was going on. I didn't want to add fuel to the fire.

I drummed my fingers on my desk, thinking about how to salvage this. Maybe she could come anyway? Somehow I wasn't sure if she'd love sitting in the corner on her own while I ran around, making sure the food was hot, but I could throw it out there. Maybe she'd like to join my family for our celebration after? Mom always did make the best turkey, and she even bought all the desserts, giving me a break for the day.

I debated the timing all day, wondering if I would come across as the creepy dude if I stopped by her work, and deciding, yes, I doubtlessly would. Double for showing up at her door unannounced. I'd probably get the police called on me for that one. Finally, thinking of June's words from last week, I decided on the good old-fashioned phone call. No hiding behind screens this time for either one of us. Besides, I never got the chance to tell her my—I mean June's—idea of using my kitchen to help disadvantaged youth learn a new skill, with seniors helping out as well. I felt hecka guilty about that, too. I meant to the night I dropped by with Thai food, but we ended up in bed before I even brought up the idea.

Finally, when I knew her store would be closed, and she had enough time to head home, I picked up the phone to call her, hoping she might be willing to meet up for a drink so I could break it to her that I needed to cancel on our Christmas Eve plans.

17

MARIA

The phone buzzed by my elbow. It was a wonder I could even hear it, considering it was buried under stacks of papers, books, and highlighters. As Eminem so eloquently reminded us, we only had one shot, one opportunity in life sometimes, and though he recommended to blow it, I decided that the first half of the lyric was quite enough. I would *not* blow this final. If I got a mediocre grade on it, which counted for half of my entire grade, I could give my chances of getting a letter of recommendation from Professor Jones a big, fat, sloppy kiss goodbye.

It could only be one of two people since Luci was a smart enough woman not to bother me during this study time. She already sent a box of Insomnia Cookies and a box of Awake tea, along with a note to let me know if she or Alex could help quiz me. I appreciated the gesture, and scarfed the cookies while they were still warm, but Advanced Principles of Neurosciences and Clinical Psychopharmacology was something I had to tackle on my own. Better to blast Christmas Pop music to remind me that yes, indeed, there was life going on outside of books and highlighters and some people were enjoying this time of year, as hard as that was for me to imagine.

Gabriel. I wasn't sure whether to be excited that it wasn't yet again my mother, or dread because I knew what I needed to do. The thing I had been trying to avoid for days. Breaking it off. As tempting as ghosting him would be, it was a cop out, a selfish move that only served to make me feel better. *Huh*, I thought to myself as I accepted the call. *I guess I did learn something in class this semester.*

"Hey Maria." Gabriel's voice was gruff with what sounded like exhaustion and my heart fell for what I was about to do. I chewed on what was left of a nail. I glanced down at my fingers. I would definitely need to put a new set on before I left the house tomorrow.

"Hi Gabriel." I wanted to go on, but my throat constricted. If Gabriel noticed anything was amiss, he didn't mention it.

"I was wondering if you were free for a drink tonight?"

The offer annoyed me more than it should. But I couldn't help it as I glanced at my kitchen table, the entire thing filled with papers and books that I needed to somehow imprint on my brain in the next week. And not to memorize but to truly understand it. His invitation seemed to highlight the differences between us. His carefree, happy-go-lucky attitude, and my desperate sprint toward a PhD and a different life than what I had growing up. *Must be nice to have all the time in the world to knock off and grab a drink any old time you want*, I figured, ignoring the niggling thought that over the last few weeks, I hadn't told him otherwise for myself. Or that I was being unfair considering the poor guy has to get up to go to work so early.

"Maria?" Gabriel asked, and I suddenly realized the thoughts whirling in my head had gone on a lot longer than I meant.

"No thank you," I managed to get out politely. Stiffly. "I have a lot to do."

"I hear that," he agreed. "Work, work, work. Which leads me to say... I have horrible news. I have to cancel our Christmas brunch, but I was hoping to make it up to you if you wanted to join me—"

My stomach dropped to my toes. I had been so excited about our Christmas Eve plans and had even been poking around the internet a bit, trying to find a reasonably priced yet simple gift I could bring with for him. Well. That was forty-five minutes I wasted where I could have been studying, wasn't it? I cut him short, blinking back the tears before I could hear his grand plan to make up the one thing I had looked forward to this holiday season.

I capped my highlighter in irritation. I was using a green one to at least bring a little holiday cheer into my place. "Gabriel, where do you see yourself in five years?" I blurted out before I realized what I was saying. It caught me by surprise, but only the fact I asked. The actual question had been on my mind since I met him.

"Where do I want to be?" Surprise filled his tone. Can't say I blamed him. I sounded like an HR manager.

"Yes, like a job." Now that I said the question out loud, I had to see it through. Had to answer the question for myself.

"I guess working at my bakery? I don't have any plans to leave it." The confusion in his voice grew, but the confusion in my mind eased. I shook my head, the fog from the last month clearing up.

Gabriel didn't want more than fun nights and late night drinks. I couldn't handle the idea of ending up with a man like one of my stepdads. I couldn't give someone a life full of fun and easy and late night drinks, at least at this point in my life. I was already signed up for years of study. Needed to guard myself and make myself as tough as nails so I can be successful and not turn into my mom. Sure, Gabriel was wonderful, one of the sweetest men I ever met, but we were simply incompatible. Maybe I had to remember his insistence the other day via our text bantering that the Backstreet Boys were better than NSYNC. Someone that drastically inaccurate could be wrong about other things, too.

I sighed over the line.

"What's wrong?" Now his voice took on a concerned tone in addition to confused. I imagined his mouth displaying a slight frown instead of the smile I had grown to adore, and my heart broke a little. I opened my mouth to explain, but then saw another call flash up on the screen, and irritation filled my chest. My mother. Well, she'd just have to wait, wouldn't she? I stabbed at the screen to send her to voicemail and carried on with Gabriel.

"This. This is what's wrong," I said, gesturing to the table in front of me. Maybe I'd make more sense if we were on FaceTime instead of a regular call, but I went on. "I can't do this anymore."

"Do what?" He sounded clipped now, the words taking on a harder sound. Harder than I've ever heard it. My stomach plummeted like it was on a roller coaster free fall.

"See you." I closed my eyes and summoned all my strength to go on. Gabriel would never understand. "We're in different worlds, Gabriel. You have this picture-perfect Instagram family, and I have, well, a sort of family. You want to bake, and I am embarking on an incredibly hard journey, trying to get accepted into the PhD program. I can't handle the stress of it all. The imbalance."

"What do you mean you have 'sort of a family'? I thought you had your mom in town? And stepdad? And what program?" His voice was more and more bewildered. I couldn't even blame him. I led himself, and myself, down this little fantasy that I had a normal family like him. Kept everything in me bottled up and deliberately didn't share details about myself so I could pretend, even for a couple short weeks, that I was carefree. Refused to let myself get close to him for this exact reason. Heck, I didn't even tell him I was working on my PhD application portfolio. Talking about that stuff was scary because the acceptance rate to the program was so low. My mind flashed to my mom. I probably had heard about fifty different dreams of hers on how she was going to strike it rich, do something exciting, or land a great job. And none of them actually happened. I knew better than to count my chickens before they hatched. Much better to create an egg of steel around yourself.

I sniffed. Oh crap, if I started crying now, my eyes would be super puffy tomorrow. I got up and started to rummage in the freezer to see if I had any frozen veggies to put on my eyes in case.

"I do. But I avoid them as much as possible, Gabriel. Not everyone has a loving family like yours. I tried to be part of your world. Just like the Little Mermaid. But I don't have legs, I have flippers."

Gabriel fell silent, and I was wondering if he was working out whether or not I had been hitting the spiked eggnog a little too hard. "Okay..."

I didn't have time for this, I thought as I snatched frozen peas out of my freezer. If I started to cry, I'd end up in front of the TV all night, eating ice cream, and I simply didn't have time for that. "Just trust me on this one, Gabriel. I need to go. I need to study my ass off for the next seven days straight, then stay up all night to get the East Village Outreach outline finished if I want any chance at a future."

"I gotta go." I clicked off without waiting for an answer and burst into the tears I so desperately tried to avoid.

18

GABRIEL

I scanned the order list in front of me. I had exactly one week to bake over a hundred of my special cakes and create a catering spread worthy of all the people at East Village. Throw in a few other orders, and keeping the bakery up and running, and it would be another seventy-hour workweek for me before I mercifully got off Christmas Eve. And even then, I would be partially working at the East Village brunch. But at least that one would be fun, as fun as it could get, I guess.

Good. Any distraction was welcome these days, even if it was long hours at the bakery. Kept me from ruminating on the disastrous call with Maria.

Maria. Just her name made me pause despite my busy day. I stood there, with my palms on the flour bin, trying to breathe out the slight heaviness in my chest.

"Uh, you okay, boss?" I was jolted back to reality by Mykenna, who stood there with the two friends she rustled up to help me get through this extra busy week. "Because, if you're like, not, we can come back."

I shook my head. "No, I'm fine. Let me show you around." I took the next half hour to assign them work. The scrawny, nervous boy I put up front with Mykenna. He could assist with bagging pastries. I asked the other, a strong looking girl, if she'd be okay helping me in the kitchen. I looked around the large, sterile environment where we'd be working for the next several hours. Too quiet. I grabbed my phone and flicked through the playlists.

"Mind AC/DC?" I asked her.

She gave me a funny look before shaking her head. Probably wondering why I didn't put on Christmas music. Well. I wasn't in the Christmasy mood. The sounds of AC/DC would match my mood perfectly today, but that was the last thing I wanted to do was pour my heart out to a high school girl. She'd probably run out the door to her parents, and I wouldn't blame her a bit.

We worked in relative ease and silence outside the blaring sound of *"Hell's Bells"* and *"Back in Black"*, which suited me fine, until Mykenna poked her head in the kitchen.

"Boss?" I began to wonder if Mykenna even knew I *had* a first name. "Someone's here to see you."

I checked my watch and saw it was past lunch already. Someone organizing the East Village brunch was supposed to come by to check the menu. I nodded and wiped my hands on my apron, telling the kids to make themselves a sandwich and take a break when they got a chance. I grabbed the proposed menu I printed out this morning and went out to the cafe, where I saw a vaguely familiar looking woman bundled up in a hat and scarf, standing by the counter.

"Hi, are you here with East Village?" I tried to remember the name Simon gave me. Lacy, I thought it was.

She nodded, and I stuck out my hand. She stared at me for a moment, eyes slightly bugged out, and shook it.

"You're Gabriel!" Her gasp of astonishment made me cringe internally. She must have read about me in some write-up or another, and I began to get self-conscious. I hoped she wasn't some kind of food groupie that made things like my James Beard award into something bigger than it was. I mean, I was proud of all my awards and even displayed them in my office, but it wasn't like I was an Oscar winning actor or anything.

Deciding to turn my embarrassment into something else, I nodded and pointed to the display case. "Did you want to try anything? I could grab you a slice of my signature cake. Or my Poire belle Hélène is quite nice if you want a dessert after dinner tonight." Quite nice was an understatement. I won multiple awards with those dang pears. Took me nine months to perfect the recipe, too. All to be eaten in under nine minutes. Sometimes the irony killed me.

She startled. "You baked them?"

I began to wonder what in the heck was going on here. Or if this person was all there. "Yeah. Why?" I asked cautiously. For a split second, I considered telling her that Poire belle Hélène pears aren't really baked, but decided to keep it short. She didn't seem like one of the food groupies that came in, trying to flirt and ask what new recipe I had up my sleeve, but then again, what did I know? I hated having my name and picture in the paper for that very reason. Always seemed like some women took it as an invitation to come by the bakery, like I might fall at their feet because they knew I won some award.

"But I thought the owner of this pâtisserie was doing the catering for East Village. Personally. And isn't he some kind of fancy French bakery genius?"

I took a few steps back from her and gave a little twirl. I pointed my toe for effect for this strange lady. Too bad I hated wearing a baker's hat, I mused. At least I still had on my white coat. Gave a better visual and all, though I'm not sure I'd call myself fancy.

"At your service, ma'am." *Sheesh*. I knew I was young, and most people expected me to be older based on my success, but come on. This woman was taking fangirling over some baked goods to a new level. I just liked playing with flour and butter. Always had, ever since I was old enough to reach the countertop as a kid.

"Yes. Gabriel Johnson, owner, head baker, accountant, marketer, and well, everything else of this fine pâtisserie establishment. How may I help you today?" I took an exaggerated bow. Hopefully, that would answer all her questions and we could get to the point. The faster the better with this woman, it seemed like.

"But Maria said you were a cake baker! I thought you, I don't know, worked at the grocery store frosting cakes or something." She glanced around wildly. "Why did you name it Spruce Pâtisserie?"

"Uh, it's my mom's maiden name. Named it after her. Sounds better than Johnson Pâtisserie, don't you think?" I asked as my mind spun wildly. *Maria?* What did she have to do with the East Village holiday brunch?

"Wait a minute. I saw you before! You were in East Village the first time I ever saw Maria. Did she send you here? Why would she? She hates me." My mind whirled, speculating if this was another weird trick.

"She does not hate you," the woman in front of me sighed. She rubbed her eyes.

"You didn't hear her phone call." I wondered why I was even going down this path. I pulled out the menu, intent on keeping it business-like. The last thing I needed this week was to examine the psyche of a woman who dumped me. I'd be doing that plenty right before I went to sleep and could do without ruminating during business hours too.

"Heard enough. I'm Luci. Maria is my bestie."

Ah. I stepped back. Well. That gave me plenty of information. I didn't need to be caught up in this hot mess. Maria made it clear she had no interest in me, and that was that. "Here's the menu," I offered to her, formally instead of addressing what she said. "Do you want to go over it?" I prayed the answer was no, that she'd trust my judgment.

"No. I want to talk about Maria."

Dang it. Even worse. I was already behind at work today, and having thoughts of her beautiful smile dance through my head would just distract me.

"Well, I don't." I crossed my arms like a toddler. We stared at each other for a few seconds. I knew Grandpa's tricks would come in handy one day.

Unfortunately, it seemed like Luci knew them as well since we sat there for a good thirty seconds. "Maria taught me all her psychology tricks," Luci taunted me. "You aren't going to win this."

I raised my eyebrow at her. "Psychology tricks?" The only psychology tricks I knew about were Grandpa's, who used them for sport.

She threw me a withering glance. "Like you don't know."

"I don't know!" I repeated back, but in a different tone. Mine was defensive.

"Maria dumped you because she's drowning in work. She's trying to pull off this project, work, school, and get her portfolio ready for her PhD application. *In Psychology.* She got a bad grade and things started to slide when you guys hung out too much. Now she's all gloom and doom, study study study."

"Why didn't she tell me this?" It suddenly made so much sense. Her heavy workload and stress, her analytical mind. Despite my hurt, I started to feel bad for her. She must be stressed to the max with all her responsibilities. "She said she was in grad school, but when I asked what program, she told me it was a clinical one. I thought it was, like pre-med or something."

Luci shrugged. "I think she keeps it under wraps. Afraid in case it doesn't work out, and doesn't get accepted into the program she's worked so hard toward. Like right now, she's struggling with some clinical psycho-something class."

My mind whirled again and again. "She needs help?"

Luci nodded. "But more than that, she needs time. Time to study and get things sorted. So if you distract her before finals…" She put her hands on her hips and narrowed her eyes at me.

I took a step back, terrified of what she was about to say. The look in her eyes told me it wouldn't be good. She leaned closer. "I'll stomp on all your cakes and leave you a bad review on Yelp."

I winced. I could handle the Yelp review. People left crappy reviews all the time. My personal favorite was the one who rated a chocolate cake one star because he wanted vanilla but his wife insisted on the chocolate. But stomping my cakes? That would make a grown man cry.

"I will leave her alone," I promised, careful to emphasize the word 'I'. Because I had a plan.

19
MARIA

"How's the studying going?" Luci leaned up against the doorframe, a white peppermint mocha in hand, right at closing time. "By the way, I got one of these too. It's disgusting. Regular chocolate is better."

I immediately dropped my highlighter at the sight of the paper cup. "Gimme," my arm shot out toward her. "Is it—"

"Yes," she cut me off before I could ask her how many shots of espresso. "I'm not suicidal."

I took a grateful sip. "What do I owe the pleasure of this surprise treat?"

"Just thought I'd come say hi. I know you're stressed to the hilt." Next to my elbow, on top of my open textbook, landed a white paper bakery bag. Stamped on it were the words *Spruce Pâtisserie*. "Got you a snack, too."

I narrowed my eyes at her. "You *didn't*." Luci was supposed to be my best friend. If she went on a one woman mission to fix things between me and my non-boyfriend, I'd be pissed. Girl code.

She opened the bag and helped herself to a macaron. "Not on purpose. Turns out the bakery is doing a bunch of the catering for the East Village brunch. I stopped by to get the menu because, as *you know,* I'm running the party. And I ran into him."

I dug through the bag myself to see what she brought, justifying it by thinking just because I dumped him, didn't mean I had to dump his baking skills.

"I don't want to hear it," I warned her. "But you better not have told him to chase after me. This is *not* one of those Hallmark Christmas movies where the man chases the woman and shows her the meaning of Christmas and all that gooey fuzzy stuff. Besides, strike one? Those movies are usually set in small towns and we live in the city. Strike two is that the man is usually the go-getter in those films, and the woman is there to show him the true meaning of life by slowing down." I took a bite of a raspberry macaron. Dear God, it was amazing. I had no idea that his bakery sold all these things since I only went that one time with him after hours.

"Strike Three. All those movies end at Christmastime, and I have a crushing workload that extends into New Year's, Valentine's Day, St. Patrick's Day, Easter, Memorial Day, then..." I stopped, trying to think of a holiday in June. Luci smirked, probably waiting to see what I'd come up with. "Then whatever," I finished lamely, right before I remembered Juneteenth. Dang it. Can't believe I stumbled on that one.

"Don't worry. I told him that if he bothered you at this time of year, I'd smush all his cakes. Then his balls."

I gasped. "You said *what?*"

"Fine. I didn't say balls, but I did tell him I'd leave a bad review on Yelp."

"Good," I grumbled. Not that it would affect him directly, but maybe his boss would have questions. I reached into the bag to see what else she brought. I hadn't been eating properly in the last week.

"BUT..."

Crap. I should have known I'd never get off that easily with her. I stuffed a big bite of croissant in my mouth. "But what?" I asked around a full mouth.

"Gross." She made a face. *"But* you asked what you owe me for the pleasure of these treats. And my answer is that you owe Gabriel another chance. I don't think he's who you think he is."

I was already shaking my head. "Doesn't matter. He could be Ryan Reynolds himself, and I'd have to turn him down. I don't have room for him in my life. Room for any man. My life to-do list is way too long."

The next words were harder to admit. The core of all my fears. "I can't become my mother, Luci," I almost whispered. My mind flashed to memories of us over the years, especially at Christmas. The years without a tree, or even a holiday dinner. The year that Stepdad #2 got drunk and destroyed our presents. The three different times we were evicted in the winter and we had to move in the middle of the night. I loved my mom for her optimism, always positive her good fortune would be right around the corner, but dang. I couldn't live like that another minute.

"I left home at seventeen for a reason, Luci." A tear snaked down my face, and I wiped it away with the back of my hand.

She leaned over and hugged me. *"And you never will, Maria.* You are not your mother. You are smarter, bolder, and savvy all around. But you can't close yourself off from life because you had a bad experience. Heck, when we met a couple of years ago, you didn't have any friends."

It was true. Luci was the first friend I made as an adult. I spent most of my life not wanting to depend on anyone for anything. Money. Emotional support. Friendship. I was always disappointed in the end, and it was easier to handle things myself. Put on a gilded look to the world as a successful, polished future psychologist with no vulnerabilities. Till Luci came into Bon Marche one day and bulldozed her way into my heart. She had tried to capture some dickhead's attention, and I had to talk her into seeing the love of her life was right in front of her, Alex. My psychology classes came in handy that day.

"Not everything in life is an addition, Maria. You can add without subtracting your time. It's called multiplying."

I lifted my eyebrow at her. "I'm not following your math lesson there. Might need to ask Alex to review it for content."

She swatted my arm, almost jostling my drink. "You know what I mean. When I came along, did I cut into your life?"

I shook my head reluctantly, knowing what she was getting at. That with the right person, life got easier, not a burden.

"That's right, I didn't. I *added* to your life. Took away some of the stress. Helped you out, supported you, and," she gestured to the counter in front of her, "making sure you were fed. Who isn't to say Gabriel couldn't be that to you? Did he ever give you an indication he wanted to subtract from your life, like all your stepdads did to your mom? Or did you project that onto him?"

I started sorting shopping bags by size, not wanting to answer her question. Just then, my phone started buzzing, and I glanced at it. My mom. Of course. Perfect timing. I chucked it back in my bag, letting it ring. Luci watched the expression on my face.

"Yep. Called it." She nodded, and I could see the flash of sympathy in her eyes. "So, back to the original question. How can you repay me? By maybe opening yourself up to the gorgeous man who baked these gorgeous treats for us."

I hesitated, knowing she might have had a point. "But I was awful to him."

"Yes, you were. But maybe he'd understand you were under a bunch of stress. *If you opened yourself up to tell him.*"

I nodded slowly. "Maybe. I just can't right now. Not in the

next week. Can I have time to think about it? I need to get through the finals this week, and turn in the project proposal to Simon. Then I'll have time to breathe until the next semester starts."

She twisted her mouth disapprovingly. "After finals, we're having this conversation again."

"After finals," I promised, hoping she'd long forget by then, though the look on her face said she'd be entering a reminder in her phone as soon as I was out of eyesight.

20

GABRIEL

Gabriel: Gramps, I'm on my way and need a favor.

I shoved my phone in my pocket without waiting for an answer and ran to my car, which for the small, small price of two thousand bucks, was finally back from the shop. I grimaced, remembering the cost as I punched the seat warmers the second I got in and watched as the flashy dashboard in front of me lit up. It was a far cry from the bakery van I had been driving around for the last two weeks. Crud. No wonder Maria thought I was a delivery driver with murderous intentions on our first date. She asked a few other questions about me, and in true-to-me form, I answered her modestly, playing down my successes.

None of that mattered right now, though. I was on a mission.

My Audi quickly cut through the roads to East Village, making it in record time. I needed to get back as soon as possible, being that it was the weekend before Christmas and orders were through the roof. But this was more important than any cake I could ever bake.

I parked and headed to the glass doors, reflecting on the first time I saw Maria. Even bundled up for the cold weather, she had glowed with elegance and charm. But that was only her outside look. Inside, she was ambitious. Funny. Soft. Even if she didn't like to show that last part. Well, if she ever talked to me again, that was up to her. I only wanted to get her the help she needed. Someone like her deserved all the good things in life, and then some.

❄

I rapped on Grandpa's door.

"Come in," a voice floated from behind the door, but not Grandpa's voice. I heard the deadbolt turn in the lock, and I stepped inside. Grandpa and June were on the couch, sharing a blanket. I tilted my head toward them and tapped my lips with my finger.

"What, boy, it's cold out," Grandpa said, taking great care to click off the app he used to unlock the door as he avoided looking at me. "June has Hulu, and I have Netflix. Sometimes we need to share."

"I didn't ask," I said, smiling triumphantly. "You jumped to conclusions on what I was wondering. Maybe I was wondering if you wanted to order burritos." Ha, take *that,* Grandpa. Oldest trick in the psychology world, confessing before I asked. Really, Grandpa should have known better. Old man was slipping around the presence of his lady.

"How's that young lady of yours, Gabriel?" June hurried to change the conversation. *Ha, got them again*, I thought to myself, coming up with a scheme. I could play wingman to Grandpa. Get him back for the times he did it to me.

I dropped my coat on the armchair next to them and perched on the edge of the seat. "That's why I'm here. Sort of. She dumped me, but I found out she needs help."

They listened as I explained the situation, at least as much as I knew from Luci.

"Maria's struggling with a class in her Psychology master's program. Didn't have time to study for it, and is nervous about her GPA and portfolio." Grandpa looked intrigued already, and I reached for my phone where I typed down the name. "Sounds complicated. Clinical Psychopharmac...pharmacistic...—"

Grandpa cut me off. "Clinical Psychopharmacology. Easy. It's about the principles and scientific data coupled with clinical practices to determine individual psychopathology needs across various mental states."

June and I looked at each other, then stared at him. "Yeah, Gramps, you're gonna need to dumb that down for me. By like ninety-eight percent."

He sighed. "Study of medications that treat mental disorders."

"You know this stuff?" Hope rose in my chest.

He scoffed. "Know it? I taught it for many years. Authored a few papers on it too."

"Think you could tutor Maria?"

"Could I help Maria," he grumbled. "Could Bill Gates show someone how to use Microsoft Word?"

I broke out into a grin. "Well. Bill Gates might have a few more billions than you. But," I said, casting my eye toward June mischievously. I raised my voice a notch. "You *do* have your health, retirement accounts, *and* a really good Medicare plan. Up to date AARP card, too, right Grandpa? And I think you even have triple A," I added at the end, figuring another acronym wouldn't hurt. Hey, Grandpa insisted on helping *me* with his mediocre wingman skills, it was time he learned that payback was a bitch.

He glared at me. I grinned innocently back.

"How can I help her?" he asked.

"I'm not allowed to contact her if I want my cakes to stay intact." I shuddered, remembering the look on Luci's face. That woman didn't play. "But you're still helping with the East Village Outreach program, getting people roused up around here, right? Maybe you can text her with updates, and slide in that, I dunno, people like you are available to mentor and tutor?" I didn't know what exactly to say. I was a baker, not an actor.

He nodded. "I'll think of something. Don't you worry."

I headed to the door, ready to get back to my stack of orders. "I never worry about you, Grandpa. Not with your health, full set of teeth, and total lack of arthritis."

21

MARIA

A strange number popped up on my phone right as I was finishing my closing tasks. I quickly copied it into Google but didn't get any hits that I recognized, so hit 'decline'. It rang again, and I debated answering, finally accepting the call in case it was Mom or something important. Usually telemarketers didn't call back twice in a row.

"Hi, is this Maria?" a vaguely familiar voice came across the line.

"Yes," I answered cautiously, shutting down the computer and grabbing my jacket as I tried to place the voice. *Oh no.* Was this Mom's new boss? Did Mom list me as an emergency contact? Did she not show up at her job again? Just when she landed a halfway decent one as a waitress at a high-end restaurant, with the promise of getting good tips. *Dang it.* Just what I needed.

"This is Paul Johnson from East Village. I was wondering if you had time to talk about the outreach project tonight. After talking to a few of my neighbors, I put together a list of potential ideas to add, centering around people who could do some mentoring in the community."

I froze. On one hand, I desperately needed it to beef up the project for Simon which was due in less than a week. On the other hand, I didn't have time to waste if I wanted to get my studying done. On the foot...

"Does this have anything to do with Gabriel?" I asked suspiciously. "Like if I show up, he won't be waiting there with poinsettias and a Santa bear or surrounded by presents for the underprivileged straight out of a rom-com Christmas movie? We won't get snowed in, and I'll find the true meaning of Christmas by sleeping in the East Village lobby by a roaring fireplace? You won't be making us pick out a Christmas tree together and decorate it?"

"There's no snow on the forecast." Paul sounded amused. "He's not around and I assure you there's no mistletoe to be found here, at least that I noticed. Meet me upstairs at East Village?"

I wavered. I suppose I could just be polite to Gabriel if I saw him for some reason. "Fine. But I only have an hour or so, then I need to get back and study."

He chuckled. "I don't think that will be a problem."

❄

THANKFULLY, Paul was there at a table, by himself, as promised when I arrived half an hour later. I glanced around in case Gabriel was hiding in the bathroom or something before I unraveled my scarf and sat down.

"Thanks for meeting me, Maria. Here's the list I compiled of people who live here who would be happy to join a mentor program. I think there's enough mentoring with high school students and the like, so I'm proposing mentorships amongst college students and fresh grads."

He slid a piece of paper with about twenty names on it, with their expertise listed next to them. I began to wonder why he couldn't have emailed me this list and saved me the time. I scanned the paper out of politeness. One lady was a retired state judge, another was a teacher, and a man had been a very successful contractor. I ran my finger down the list until I saw the name *Paul Johnson - interpreting existing theory and research in psychology* and froze. I recognized that name. I just didn't put it all together, being that the last name Johnson was so common.

"You're Dr. Johnson," I said dully, feeling a flush creep from my cheeks to the top of my hairline. My thoughts were swirling, wondering how I could have been so stupid. Dr. Johnson was legendary at my university. He had been the dean for over twenty years and taught some of the most complicated Clinical Psychology classes in the program. Heck, I had several books he authored as required reading. Probably passed his picture hanging in the hallway a hundred times without really looking at it. Even more than that, he was Gabriel's grandfather. Gabriel, who I dumped for thinking he was only a guy out for a good time.

Dr. Johnson—now that I knew who he was, I suddenly had a hard time thinking of him as simply *Paul*— sensed what I was feeling. "Yes. Gabriel didn't quite follow in my footsteps. Preferred Le Cordon Bleu over a PhD."

I winced at his underlying message. Le Cordon Bleu? I wasn't much in the kitchen, but even I had heard of one of the best baking schools on the planet. "In Paris?" I asked, afraid of the answer. But I already knew. In my snobbery, I pegged him as being anti-ambitious. Never in my wildest imagination did I allow for the scenario of him trotting off to the other side of the world to learn to bake amongst the finest in the field. An endeavor that probably put my own to shame.

Dr. Johnson nodded. "The very one. He always was good with flour and sugar."

Well, if I didn't feel like a big enough pile of crud fifteen seconds ago, those words certainly sealed the deal. My skin crawled with disgust with myself. Disgust that I put up a front for him. Disgust that I judged him and created a false story of who and what I thought he was based on his profession.

I started to rise from my chair. "Thank you for this," I said formally. I was desperate to get home and think about all I did to Gabriel. Or, alternatively, hide under a rock till the end of time. That sounded even better. "I'll take a look."

"Maria. Please stay." Dr. Johnson's eyes told me he noticed my discomfort.

That's all it took for me to drop back into my chair. Embarrassed as I was, no way was I going to disrespect a man with Dr. Johnson's accomplishments.

"Gabriel mentioned you might need help with your schoolwork. Is there something I can assist you with?"

His face was kind, but it would be like asking Ed Sheeran to sing me *"The Itsy Bitsy Spider"*. Which come to think about, would be pretty kick-ass. I wouldn't turn that opportunity down. But still. How in the heck did Gabriel know? There was only one explanation... *Luci,* and I couldn't decide whether to kiss her or kill her. Maybe both.

"I'm a little lost on Clinical Psychopharmacology. And Advanced Principles of Neuroscience," I hated to admit out loud. "I got behind with all I've been working on lately." I wasn't going to admit the other reason I got behind, but I had a pretty good idea he knew anyway.

He shook his head. "It would be an honor to help you. If you'll accept."

If I would accept. This would be like training for the Olympics and turning down the gold medal at the end.

"If you don't mind," I said in a rush. "I'll cancel everything. Anything. I'll work around your schedule." I may as well have told him I'd bow down in praise at the sight of him. Which wouldn't be that far off the truth at this point.

He laughed, displaying a wide grin that I had seen before. On Gabriel. A pang of missing him went through me even as relief in getting the help I needed surged through my veins, making me feel almost weak. "That won't be necessary. I'm retired. You have time now? And who is your professor, anyway?"

"Professor Jones," I said glumly at the thought of her. I pulled out my laptop, not one to look a gift horse in the mouth. One must strike when the iron is hot, or when the renowned professor offers to tutor you in a subject he probably helped herd into the modern era.

"*Her?* She's still around? I hired her when she came on board." He laughed at some memory. "Don't be afraid of her," he said with a conspiratorial look. "I know for a fact she only got a C in this class. And we're going to one up you for her."

I grinned, feeling buoyed for the first time in weeks. I still had plans to maim Luci and Gabriel, but for now, opening myself up wasn't turning out too badly.

22

GABRIEL

I was back to whistling while I worked, and this time it was even Christmas songs. Mykenna and her friends were probably dang relieved that my Spotify playlist now consisted of Christmas music by Kelly Clarkson and Justin Bieber instead of the heavy metal tunes that suited me better a few days ago.

Grandpa remained tight-lipped but told me he had been working with Maria, setting up a guide and working through explanations on things I didn't understand and likely never would. Never wanted to, for that matter. He said the studying was going well, and that was enough to put me in the holiday mood. Even if Maria never talked to me again, I could go out happy knowing that she was one step closer to her dreams.

My one regret was that I never got around to telling her my idea about using the bakery to work with disadvantaged teens to help them toward a potential career path.

I had also mentioned it to Grandpa last night when he called.

"I could float it by her," he offered.

I thanked him but declined. We ended things on a pretty

crappy note, with me canceling on her. I was upset at the time, but now I understood a little bit more. She probably thought I was just another person in a long lineup of people who let her down. She didn't need my distractions this week. Heck, it was probably too much work to put together anyway, knowing that the final proposal was due to Simon in just a few days.

"Hi Gabriel," a familiar voice came across the counter. I looked up and recognized June. Standing next to her was a beautiful blonde.

"Hey, June," I said, walking around the front and leaning up against the display case. "Whatcha up too?"

"Just a little last-minute Christmas shopping," she said, waving her hand in the air. "My granddaughter Elise and I figured we'd stop in for a couple of croque monsieurs." She nudged her granddaughter toward me in a move I recognized. It was obvious that June and Grandpa had been conniving again.

I suppressed a grin as I stuck my hand out in greeting to Elise. At any other time in the world, I'd be very interested in getting to know the beautiful, curvy blonde in front of me. But these days, I knew the Christmas angel I wanted was a feisty brunette.

"Two croque monsieurs coming up. On the house, of course. Because I don't charge for my grandfather's lady friend."

June giggled, giving me the answer that Grandpa had been evading for weeks. *Gotcha, Grandpa.* I couldn't wait to rub it in his face next time.

"I'll run to the ladies room and be right back," she promised, leaving me and Elise together. I cut to the back counter and started assembling the sandwiches.

"Sorry about that," Elise said shyly. "I tried to tell her that Panera would be fine, but she insisted on coming here, and now I think I know why."

"Don't worry about it," I said, sliding a few peppermint and vanilla macarons on a plate for good measure. "She and my Grandpa have a thing going, though he won't admit it to me. He's always up in my business, too."

"I get it. Grandma always wants me to find what she calls a 'nice young man' to settle down with. Even though I tell her it doesn't work that easily." Elise rolled her eyes, but she was smiling. "Too hard to find someone good and genuine who doesn't have all sorts of women sliding into his DMs. Not that I think you're that type of guy," she added hastily.

I smiled. "I'm not. Know them though." I finished assembling the sandwiches and added them to the griddle. Elise was beautiful. Sweet. Vetted by June, which would usually be a plus, even if it *was* her granddaughter. But...

"I'll be honest with you. I'm still a little hung up with someone I just dated." Elise was beautiful and if she was June's granddaughter, she already had my stamp of approval. But I just couldn't shake the image of Maria, and the spark that came between us every time we were together.

Elise nodded knowingly. "I could tell."

"How so?" I asked, shocked. I glanced down. As far as I knew, I wasn't wearing a shirt that said *Call me, Maria!*

"You had a faraway look in your eyes when Grandma introduced us." Elise grabbed the napkin I held out to her. "What's she like?"

I thought for a second. Maria was all the things, but it was hard to narrow it down to only a few adjectives. "Beautiful. Determined. Smart as heck. And hard as heck to open up. I want to reach out again, but not sure how. I let her down on some plans she was excited about."

Elise watched me pull the sandwiches from the griddle and place them on plates. "It's easy. Give her a reason to trust and believe in you."

As I handed her the sandwiches, I realized she was absolutely right. That's the one thing Maria was missing in her life. People to trust and believe in. Outside Luci, who by all accounts, seemed like a loyal friend, I couldn't tell if she had many people to rely on in her life. Which was probably a sign right there.

With a sinking feeling, I understood that I could be lumped into that second category. Sure, we had fun, but what had I delivered to her that was more than a good time and a couple presents? I asked Grandpa to tutor her, which was great and all, but that was easy. Required almost no effort on my part. Even worse, I had promised to help her work on the East Village Outreach project, and we never got around to it outside of some vague talks. As far as I knew, she had some parties and tutoring on the plan. Not the most robust.

I had a sudden burst of inspiration. "Mykenna? I need your help if you have a few minutes," I called toward the back.

"Sure, boss," a voice called back. I winced. I really was going to need to make sure she knew I had a real first name. But I could worry about that later.

First things first, though. I skidded to the table where June and Elise were sitting. Elise was shaking her head, and June had a slightly disappointed look on her face. I pretended not to notice.

"Hey June?" I was tempted to start humming "Hey Jude", but stopped myself, figuring she probably heard it about a million times in her life already.

June looked at me, slightly disapproving. Well. What I was going to say next would cheer her up. "Yes, dear?"

I put my hands on the table and leaned in a little. "I know the way to impress Grandpa for Christmas."

Despite herself, I knew I had hooked her. "Go on."

I pulled out my phone and pulled up a link for a present I was going to order for him. I hated to give up the best Christmas present idea for him I've ever seen but this was more important. Talk about taking one for the team.

"See this?" I slid the phone across the table her way.

She wrinkled her nose. "Who would wear a Christmas sweater with Kelly Clarkson's face on it?"

"Grandpa. And if you're fast enough, you can get this with express delivery." Another inspiration struck me. "Stay right there."

I jogged over to the garland draped on the far wall that Mykenna had hung up a few weeks ago. Standing up on a chair, I tugged off the mistletoe in the center. I dropped it back off with June. "And if I'm right, which I know I am, this will give him gift number two."

Without waiting for an answer, I jogged back to the kitchen to run my idea past Mykenna.

❄

Luckily, she loved it. "This is really sick, boss," she said as she listened to my idea. I had taken June's original suggestion and expanded upon it.

"Um. So you like it?" I wasn't quite sure. I needed to get familiar with the Urban Dictionary app if I was going to keep hiring these high schoolers.

"Yeah. No cap."

I decided not to ask about that one. Instead, I asked her to handle any of the last minute customers while I did some work in my office.

First, I drafted out a few emails to local principals, outlining my idea of having seniors and students use my kitchen for learning opportunities, potentially helping with bake sales or even food for the homeless. I cc'd Grandpa, knowing he'd love the opportunity to rally his friends around. My next emails were to other small business friends, sending a copy of my proposal, and encouraging them to do the same. Finally, I created an outline to send to Maria, describing how we could use the bakery kitchen in the off-hours, the supplies the bakery was willing to donate, and the commitment I was likely going to be able to rustle up from people at East Village. I even added the contact information to two friends that already wrote back, a coffee roaster and lawn care owner, telling me they were in. My hope was that I could help launch some kids into learning to love baking as much as I did and get some senior citizens feeling useful again.

I typed in her email address, looking over it once more. Well, whether she liked it or not, at least she would know someone was trying for her. Rallying for her, and wanting her to succeed at putting together a plan for the program. Not to mention helping out all the people at East Village. Being able to help everyone at once was just a cherry on top.

I crossed my fingers and hit 'send', then went back to work, already knowing I'd be putting in a good eighteen-hour day today.

23

MARIA

"Wow. You look different," Luci remarked as I slid into the backseat of Alex's car. I had resolutely refused to go to the East Village Christmas brunch after Gabriel canceled on me, but Luci insisted I go with her and Alex.

"It'll be a good time," she had pleaded. "I got a classic rock cover band to play Christmas music and set up a gingerbread house making competition. Had to keep the last part on the down-low, though. Didn't want people using 3-D software to design plans before we even started."

I wanted to decline her but then thought of Dr. Johnson, who had been so helpful the last week, and my sad Christmas Eve plans, which basically revolved around Chinese takeout.

Luci saw me considering. "And let's be real. I need your help setting up, and making sure everyone gets the same number of graham crackers so there isn't gingerbread mansion making going on for some people while the others have to create gingerbread shacks."

I finally relented and agreed to go.

"How do I look different?" I asked, looking down at my outfit.

Black patent miniskirt with feather trim, red cashmere sweater, and black knee-high boots. Christmasy fun. "Is it the Santa hat?"

"No, it's the lack of bags under your eyes. New concealer?"

"Thanks, Luce. Love you, too." I blew her a sarcastic kiss, but I knew she was right. "It's a little something called...I PASSED THE GODDANG TEST WITH FLYING COLORS!"

"YES!" We screamed together.

"Ladies! I'm excited for Maria too, but can we, you know, not have me crash the car?" Luckily, Alex's voice had laughter in it.

"Sorry, Alex. I'm toooooo dang excited." I leaned back into the seat, beaming to myself. Everything seemed to fall into place in the end. With Dr. Johnson's help with one-on-one tutoring I could have only dreamed of getting, suddenly classes made sense to me. I even turned in my final East Village Outreach proposal to Simon, who loved it, and the store was closed for three days. In other words, for the next seventy-two hours, I was free to relax.

I winced. The proposal. If there was one thing to bring down my mood, it was thinking of the East Village Outreach proposal. Two days before it was due, Gabriel emailed me the most perfect idea, one that rounded out the entire program and put it over the top. Naturally, I immediately reached out and thanked him, and had even tentatively asked to get together, thinking maybe we could repair things, but he turned me down, telling me he was too busy. I couldn't even blame him. I treated him worse than finding yellow snow next to your face when making a snow angel. The only mystery is why he even wanted to do this for me in the first place. Setting me up to study with Dr. Johnson. Giving me the idea for the program, and clearing it with his boss. Did he feel guilty about how I almost lost everything in the first place? Well, that wasn't his fault. It was mine for not prioritizing correctly.

I looked out the window as Alex pulled into the parking lot. With a jolt, I saw the Spruce Pâtisserie van in the lot. *What in the heck was Gabriel doing here?* My chest tightened. He told me he had to cancel on our Christmas brunch for some other plans. Was it a lie? Did he not want to see me and made up some ruse to get me to back off? Is that why he brushed me off the other day, so he could take another woman to the brunch?

Luci saw me stare at the van with more horror than any van should invoke, save for white murder vans. She started nervously tugging on her hair, a trait I knew she did only when she was about to say something she didn't really want to.

"Maria?" her voice was small. "I have to confess something."

"Oh, do you?" My voice was tight. Alex took this as a sign.

"You know, why don't I go in and get things started. See you inside." He was gone before either of us could object.

Luci sighed. I wished I could see her face, but I was still in the backseat. "Gabriel is catering the luncheon. The original caterer bailed, and well, he was the only one we could find on short notice."

"But he's a baker," I argued, like that would make a difference. Obviously, the guy was in there, cooking up something. I could see from the side of her that Luci was biting her lip, unsure what to say next.

"*Oh nooooo.*" The realization hit me like a ton of bricks. Gabriel wasn't canceling on our Christmas Eve brunch plans because he was flaky. He was doing it to cater a special Christmas luncheon for senior citizens. And when he tried to tell me, I cut him off, thinking he was an unreliable person, like so many of my mom's boyfriends. Didn't even give him a chance to explain himself. "*Oh nooooo,*" I repeated. "Heck, I *feel* like a pile of you know what. Why didn't you tell me, Luci?" I demanded.

"Because I didn't want to jeopardize the program. Or

brunch." Her eyes pleaded with me to understand, and I did. A little. "You wouldn't have come if you knew in advance, would you? And I didn't want you to be alone on Christmas."

It would have been unlikely, I'd give her that. "Fine. I'll forgive you and enjoy myself, but I will *not* interact with him. I'll talk to you, Dr. Johnson, Alex, and if I need to, his boss or whoever is in charge of the catering."

"That's another thing," Luci said as we got out of the car and headed out into the cold, toward the door. "Gabriel, well, kind of sort of *is* the owner."

I stopped short, almost slipping on the ice. "He's *what?*" I screeched. My head started spinning again, all the pieces falling more and more into place. It all made sense now. How Gabriel always was at the bakery and gave me that weird look when he said his boss wouldn't mind me being in there after hours. How Dr. Johnson told me he went to Le Cordon Bleu. All the times he had to prioritize work. How he developed the whole bakery program for me. Gabriel wasn't just a baker. I had gone to the Spruce Pâtisserie website, where it listed all the awards won by the bakery. Won by Gabriel. Holy crap. Gabriel won more awards at his age than most people could ever have dreamed of in a lifetime. And I had judged him for not going to a college like me. By my own experiences and prejudices.

My stomach clenched like I had self-delivered a sucker punch. How could I have been so stupid? More importantly, how could I have been such a stuck-up asshat?

"Can you give me a minute?" I asked Luci stiffly. "I need to collect myself."

"Of course," she said, giving me a hug. "But don't be too hard on yourself. You were under a lot of stress."

She was right, of course, but that didn't give me an excuse to be a judgmental jerk. I sank onto a bench near an open courtyard as she hurried inside, not even feeling the cold wind whipping around me. The heat radiating from my brain was enough warmth for me.

I barely even noticed when someone slid onto the bench next to me. Whoever it was, they were crazy. Their butt was going to freeze. I could already feel mine stiffening up, which, on second thought, might not be a bad thing after all the junk food I consumed in the last week while studying.

"Hey."

Gabriel. My mind came to a screeching halt at the familiar and comforting sound of his voice. Why was he even here, after I had acted like such an asshat to him? Despite the warmth of his mere presence radiating off him and onto me like a warm hug, my entire body stiffened, if that was even more possible in this cold.

"Hi," I mumbled back. "Don't you need to go bake something?" I wiped away a discrete tear before I could freeze. "Give people cakes or cookies for lunch?"

He laughed, giving me a warmth I didn't deserve right about then. "Trust me. I'm nobody's chef. But when Simon asked me to cater, I had to pull a few recipes out from the dusty part of my brain. There will be more than cake on the table, I promise."

That lone tear alerted its friends, and the waterworks started. "Gabriel, I'm so sorry. I treated you terribly, and you did nothing but help me, and everyone else out."

Gabriel's arm went around me, and suddenly, I wanted nothing more than to cozy up to this amazing guy. I leaned in, grateful for the extra warmth.

"Don't cry." He wiped my eyes with the edge of his scarf. "You'll ruin your mascara."

I gave him a watery smile. "The tears will probably freeze before it gets to that point." I hesitated, wanting to ask the real question, and, no, nothing about his life goals. "But Gabriel, why are you always so nice to me? When I was awful to you? Refused to open up when you tried to get to know me?"

He gave a little half-shrug and looked out into the white snowy courtyard before turning his hazel eyes back toward me. "Because I saw something in you that I don't think you even knew you had. You were so caught up in being independent, and having the picture-perfect life, that you forgot people might like you for you. Want to help you for you. You're a driven, successful woman but it's hard to do it all alone."

"Be an addition, not a subtraction," I said, thinking of Luci's words from the other week. I drew in a deep breath, my heart already thumping for what I was about to say. "Gabriel, I tried to pretend everything was perfect because I wanted everything to be perfect, like your family. But I have a mom who mooches off of me and marries every man in sight, and stepdads who leech right off her by quitting their jobs and dedicating their lives to their Netflix queue. I spent my childhood trying to protect myself and my adulthood running from that lifestyle. And people don't understand what it's like when you love your mom and want to help her, but are also terrified you'll end up just like her. Only Luci has ever met her." The knot that had sat so solidly in my stomach for so long somehow seemed to unravel just a bit when Gabriel gave me a steady gaze, telling me he wasn't judging me; that he wanted to understand so he could take away some of the stress and pain.

"Yep," he said, giving my shoulders a squeeze, and smiling down on me. "I can't pretend I know your life. Just a few hints here and there. But one thing I do know is that you're worth it, and won't repeat your mother's mistakes. But I can't tell you that, you need to believe it for yourself."

I put my head on his shoulder, and he wrapped his arms around me, kissing me on the head. "You aren't her, Maria. You can love her and accept she has flaws," he murmured.

With that, he stood up, and held out his hand to help me up. "Should we go in? Before we both freeze?"

I took his hand and gladly stood up. And not just to get out of the cold. Because Luci was right. Gabriel was right. I wasn't my mother, nor did I have her lack of judgment. Letting people in wasn't a sign of weakness. In fact, letting the right people in, like Luci, Dr. Johnson, and now Gabriel, was a sign of strength.

"Before we go in though..." Gabriel pulled me close, and for the first time with him, I truly let go. Not physically, that ship already sailed, but the harder type of letting go. Emotionally. His lips brushed mine, then let them sink against so softly that I thought maybe I imagined things. I grabbed the back of his neck, and he thrust his mouth to meet mine. The heck with being delicate. I wanted to sink into this wonderful man, get to know every part of him, let him know every part of me. But first, I wanted to taste him. Remember all the things I pushed away from me over the last few weeks, not allowing them to infiltrate into my mind or emotions. It all came together in one rush as he kissed me back. A kiss full of promise, excitement, and what I now knew to be trust.

I could have stayed there all day if he didn't break away and shiver. "Hey, Maria, I love this and all, but I'm freezing my ass out here. Could we take this indoors?"

I giggled and took his hand as we made our way inside. We walked hand in hand toward the dining room where I saw Luci's face break out into a massive grin before Alex tugged her away to the gingerbread tables.

"Come help me?" he asked. "I mean, if you don't mind."

I grinned. From now on, there wasn't much he wouldn't get my help with. Like it or not, this guy was stuck with me.

Gabriel stopped short right before we got through the kitchen doorway. I turned to see what he was staring at, then I, too, started to stare. Was that *Dr. Johnson*? Wearing a sweatshirt with Kelly Clarkson on it? Was this some kind of joke? Or was this an ugly sweater party and nobody told me? Before I could ask Gabriel what in the heck was going on, Dr. Johnson glanced up at some mistletoe that was hastily taped above the doorway, then leaned in toward an older woman, and gave her a big kiss.

"I knew it, Grandpa!" Gabriel shouted. "I win!" Well. Looks like Luci wasn't the only person I knew who liked to bet on other people's love lives.

"Yes, well, Gabriel, what are you doing here?" Dr. Johnson cleared his throat.

Gabriel pointed to the kitchen. "I'm, um, catering? Have been for hours? In fact, I could point out you've been *helping* me this whole time, so this is not exactly a surprise?"

"I see..." Dr. Johnson mused. Then suddenly, he said, "Forget it, Jane. Gabriel has been right all along. I love you and it would be my honor to call you mine."

The older woman gasped and covered her face with her hands before she threw them around his neck again. "Yes, Paul."

Gabriel and I snuck around them toward the kitchen. "And don't think you're getting out of helping us, you two. As soon as you're done with the lovey-dovey stuff, I expect you right back in the kitchen," he mock ordered them.

"Aye aye, captain," Dr. Johnson gave Gabriel a mock salute in return. "Maria, can we have a quick word?"

Gabriel and Jane disappeared into the kitchen, leaving me with Dr. Johnson. "I'm very pleased to hear your test went well." Dr. Johnson reached into his pocket. "I have a little something for you."

"No," I protested. "You tutoring me was present enough. Present enough for a lifetime." Still, though, I stuck my hand out for the white envelope he was offering me.

"Open it," he nodded. "I know that you have your own letters of recommendations to get, but I thought maybe you'd like to add this to your portfolio."

With trembling hands, I read the first few lines. It was a letter, indicating that in our brief time he had gotten to know me, I proved myself a capable, intelligent woman who would succeed well as a PhD student.

Tears welled up, and this time I couldn't stop them. A letter from the former dean would be an incredible boost to my portfolio and provide me an edge I so desperately wanted. Dr. Johnson wisely patted me on the shoulder and left to give me a few moments. "It's all true, Maria," he said as he headed toward the kitchen.

Luci rushed across the room at the sight of my tears. "If that rat bastard hurt you in any way, I'm going to poison his lunch," she announced, already reaching for her phone, most likely to google where to buy arsenic on Christmas Eve.

"No, that's not it," I cried, handing her the note. She started to scan it, then threw me into a massive hug while Alex watched on. Gabriel and Jane poked their head through the door to see what was going on, and I rushed over to Gabriel to kiss him under the mistletoe.

I had one more thing to do, though, before I could immerse myself into work. Something I thought I'd never do.

"Gabriel, are you free after this? I'm going to my Mom's for Christmas Eve dinner, and I'd love to introduce you to her and my stepdad. It's not going to be much, but..." I trailed off, hoping he'd get the idea.

Gabriel leaned back to look me in the eye. "I'd love to meet the mother of the woman I love. Because hard times will always be better when we face things together. But can we stop and get her something nice on the way? I don't want to come empty-handed."

Unexpected tears sprung up, and I batted them away. I didn't need tears right now. Right now, surrounded by people who cared for me and encouraged me at every step, I knew now that despite any stress I was crushed under, I wasn't going to be alone.

❄

Thank you for reading! I hope you loved meeting Maria and Gabriel. The next book in the East Village Christmas series is *Fake Holi*date,* out now!

If you liked Get the Message, you'll enjoy the <u>Love, Lessons series</u>, starting with Love, Redefined.

<u>Love, Redefined</u>
Getting dumped sucks. What's worse is when your new coworker is your old high

AUTHOR'S NOTE

Hope you liked this book! If you did, sign up for my bi-weekly newsletter and grab a free copy of the East Village prequel novella, featuring Luci: https://dl.bookfunnel.com/aplil7mlmt

TITLES BY BRYNN NORTH

Love Lessons Series
Love, Redefined
Love, Game

Falling Unexpectedly Series
Get the Message - Head over Heels Anthology
Take Your Pick (January 2022)

East Village Christmas Novellas
Under Wraps (prequel)
Christmas Crush
Fake Holi*date

Short Stories
Going Up - Storybook Pub 2

Don't want to miss a book? Follow me:

facebook.com/AuthorBrynnNorth
instagram.com/author_brynn_north
amazon.com/author/brynnnorth

ABOUT BRYNN NORTH

Contemporary Romance & Chick Lit
with sizzle and sass

Brynn North's goal is to write fun, witty, and relatable books that leave you with a smile and laugh. Her heroines are often finding their way in life, in and out of relationships. Her characters may not always be perfect people, but hey, neither are we, right? She hopes that you can see another perspective or even parts of yourself in her books and realize you aren't alone in figuring this whole life thing out.

Her books are chick lit or closed-door romance, perfect for readers who love chemistry and sizzle but no explicit content.

She is a Minnesota native and still lives in Minneapolis with her family, loving it for approximately eight months out of the year. The other four months she dreams about moving to a warmer zip code. She is a total cat lady, with the best cats in the entire world. #sorrynotsorry

Sign up for her bi-weekly newsletter and grab a free copy of her Christmas novella here.

(FAKE) Holi*date

A CHRISTMAS ROMCOM NOVELLA

BRYNN NORTH

FAKE HOLI*DATE - CHAPTER 1

Dressed in my favorite jeans—distressed Levi's that make my butt look amazing-- and a new red sweater with snowflakes that is not quite cashmere but nicer than my usual upcycle thrift-store vintage finds, I head inside. The pom-pom on my black wool hat bounces as I walk. My black wedge booties elongate my legs as much as they can in winter. But really, how long can legs look on someone who tops out at five foot three?

Considering it's mid-December, and I'm so freaking cold, I'm dressed as cute as I can be for what is likely going to be the most important coffee meeting of my entire life. Make that the *start* of the rest of my life.

My teeth chatter away, and I look up how many calories I'm burning to see if I can shorten tonight's workout a bit. Surely I burned at least fifteen or twenty on the walk from my car to here, earning me the right to knock off the treadmill a good minute or two early?

If I could ask Santa for one small wish, it'd be that Minneapolis would miraculously do a total 180 on the temperature and turn eighty degrees. Then I could don a cute sundress and not the warmest jacket I owned, but I'll take what I can get because my ex-boyfriend, Sam, asked me to meet him. Right before Christmas, might I add. Surely this means good things. My best friend, Declan, warned me not to dive into conclusions like I usually do, but Declan is just a hater. He doesn't understand true love as I do. How can he, when he has never had a relationship last more than a few weeks?

I push through the door of the coffee shop and spot an empty table at the back of the wall. A woman is beelining to it with a paper cup of tea in each hand, and immediately I rush toward the table as fast as I can and slide my butt in. Rude? Yes. I send her a silent apology with my eyes as she stands there, glaring at me. But if only she knew this is a dire situation. I'm about to see my ex-boyfriend for the first time in months, and I need a place where I can talk to him and not huddle in the corner sipping tea while we talk over the chatter of luckier people who scored a table. She'd understand, right? Girl code and all.

I mean, sure, I stalked Sam's Facebook and Instagram accounts once or twice, trying to find any crumb of information pointing to him missing me. But I stopped after the first month, as every time I saw something new, my heart seemed to compress a bit more. Per my request, we have had no contact since the breakup. That is based on the "no contact" rule in every breakup blog post I've read, and there were many that swore will determine if we missed each other, or were meant to be. Five months later, I'm still leaning toward "meant to be," but I have no idea what Sam wanted.

Then, out of the blue, he texted me, asking me to meet up. Just the sight of his name on my phone sent my stomach spinning into overdrive, and tears welled up at the corners of my eyes. I missed him so much, much more than I allowed myself to think about, because I was trying too hard to be the cool, independent girl after our breakup.

Turns out while I maybe don't *need* him, wanting him is an entirely different story.

Sam texting me had to mean something. Maybe he was getting the holiday feels, and those, in turn, made him reconsider what he wanted. I hope.

I flash another quick apologetic smile to the woman as I sit down and pull out the white box from my purse. I didn't go wild or anything. Just baked him a little slice of his favorite Christmas cake from my Grandma Thelma's recipe. I had to beg her for the recipe and promise her up and down, right and left, that I won't post it as one of those TikTok recipe videos she loves to watch. Finally, she gave it to me, along with a strict lecture. She said if anyone is going to go viral on TikTok, it will be her, not me. I think she is already plotting out her skit and everything. Grandma is very proud of her original content, so I knew better than to mess with her. Grandma's always planning how to go viral. I'm not sure that's actually a thing you can plan, but if there is a way, Grandma's got a ten-point action plan for it.

Sam is running a bit late, so I take my compact out and powder my nose, taking a minute to smooth out my dark hair around my shoulders. It won't do to remind him of Rudolph the first time I'd seen him in months. Sam, of course, will arrive looking like he always does. Like the gorgeous former linebacker for the college football team, which is precisely what he is. Sam is beautiful, with dark hair, almost black, and brown eyes. With his broad shoulders and chiseled jawline, I had gotten used to women doing a double take when he walked past them. And for two wonderful years, I was on his arm to gloat at them. Sam was with *me*, only had eyes for *me*.

Until he didn't.

Five months. I drum my red-painted fingernails on the table to calm my nerves, thinking about it. I'm still taking our breakup pretty hard, if I'm being honest, and have spent countless nights wondering if maybe this can be something we'd recover from. Can couples really get back together after they find themselves? Maybe?

That's what he told me when we broke up, at least. Sam said we got together a little too young, and he needed to see who he really is. He was only twenty-four, and he was staring down at four years of medical school, with residency after that. It was going to be a stressful time, and he had to get his head straight before he dove in.

It's beyond me why he couldn't find out who he was while living his everyday life like the rest of us had to, but I gritted my teeth, swallowed my pride, and agreed. Besides, I knew getting ready for the MCAT and application process was bearing down on him. No wonder his head was swimming.

I clear my throat as I think this over. Thankfully, he sorted it out in time for New Year's. We could laugh about how the year ended, but how the new one will start the way it should be. *Together.*

Finally, after what seems like a billion years, I see Sam through the window. My breath rises sharply. Sam is as gorgeous as ever. Better, actually. I stare at his muscular frame as he opens the door. He has a glow about him, one I haven't seen in a long time. He looks relaxed. Happy. How one is happy and relaxed when studying for the MCAT is a mystery for the ages, but it seems to work for Sam.

Hope flutters in my chest. My mind frantically clicks through all the articles I googled this afternoon. Ones titled things like "How to Get Your Ex Back; How to Not Come Across as Desperate; Ten Topics to Talk About When You're Trying to be a Breezy Cool Chill Girl."

Any of their advice would be better than what I am doing right now, which is shooting off my chair screaming *"SAM"* for everyone in the café to hear.

Fake Holi*Date - Chapter 1

Sam's head jerks over to me. Then a smile flashes across his cheeks, showing off those dimples I love. My heart beats heavily in my chest. I can't believe it. Finally, the love of my life is back in my life. I try not to stare at him as he makes his way over to me, but fail miserably as I take in the sight of him.

"Hattie!" He reaches over and greets me with a hug before pulling back to examine me. And it takes everything in me not to bury my head into his chest, just like I've done so many times. Instead, I beam back at him. Should I kiss him? No, I decide, that's too formal, pushy even. We're just getting back on our first date after all this time. I can't do that, because he'll think I'm a crazy person. Which might be true in this case, but I need to attempt to hide it for appearances' sake.

Sam looks down at the table. "Nothing to drink? Do you want me to get it?"

I blush and bite my lip. I don't want to tell Sam, one of the nicest, most polite people I'd ever met, outside of Declan, that I almost hip-checked a woman to get the last seat at the last table. Sam laughs at my sheepish cringe, and I shiver. Every happy nerve in me dances at the sound I love so much. God, I missed him so much. But now? He's back. No, I correct myself. *We're* back.

"No worries," he says. "I'll grab something." He heads over to the counter, whistling. An actual *whistle*, and I'm pretty sure it's "Can You Feel the Love Tonight," which isn't exactly Christmassy —and come to think about it, it's afternoon, not night—but it's still enough to make me start grinning like a fool.

I wait and tap my fingertips on the box of cake as I watch him get our drinks. He still remembers my favorite order. Peppermint black tea with a hint of honey. See? We are meant to be together. A man who remembers a woman's order is a good man. I'll have to remember to tell Declan that when I talk to him. Declan always tells me Sam is clueless, but check him out, being a gentleman and ordering my favorite drink.

I gaze into Sam's deep-chocolate-brown eyes as he places my tea on the table between us. "Thank you, Sam. What a wonderful beverage on such a wintry day." There. Perfect. Casual yet not over the top. Reading those articles today did me a favor. Score one for *Cosmo*.

Sam sits down casually. I eagerly inch closer, closing the gap between us. Is this where he tells me he wants me back? Wants *us* back?

Sam pulls out an envelope from inside his leather bomber jacket. "I have something for you."

Something for me? My eyes light up. Before I can stop myself, I pull the small white cake box out from beside me. "I have something for you, too!"

He better appreciate it. It took me four hours and about a million dollars in ingredients, and a solid two hours of Grandma telling me I was doing it wrong, after all.

Declan, of course, rolled his eyes at my baking spree as he sat on Grandma's couch, watching Netflix. But, ha ha, Declan, look who is prevailing! "Don't get him anything, Hattie," Declan had urged me. I love how Declan still has a slight Irish accent even after so many years in the USA. "You should bring him some old shoes. Or something that tastes like dirty dishwater. That's what he deserves."

But Declan is wrong, isn't he? Sam is about to ask me back. What I've been dreaming about for weeks is all about to come true.

I shove the box across the table toward Sam and eagerly snatch the card. What is this? Is it some kind of declaration of love? Some *"take me back"* Christmas card? I've never seen one of those, but there is a first time for everything. Etsy has all sorts of things for sale, so surely he could have found it there if he searched hard enough.

My smile freezes as I lift the flap with my finger. Something is off about this envelope. It's thick. Has engraving on the front. I tell my racing heart this is nothing big. It's innocent. What can a little five-by-seven envelope do to anyone? Besides, of course, giving out massive paper cuts. The front of it says my name, *Hattie Martin,* in gold letters. *Calligraphy* letters.

Oh crap, this isn't good.

My stomach flip-flops as I slide the card out of the envelope. And immediately I'm as good as sucker-punched as the wind leaves my lungs with an audible *whoosh*. My mouth drops open as I stare at the piece of paper, slightly blurring with my eyes bugging out of my head now.

This is no Christmas card. Heck, I bet Sam has never even heard of Etsy, despite me selling on it for close to two years.

Sam's opening his cake box, oblivious to my almost medical emergency right in front of him, and I'm questioning what kind of doctor he'll make if he's too busy looking at cake instead of someone having a heart attack.

"Wow! Thank you. You know how much I love this cake during the holidays. I'll sure miss it."

My head spins so fast I can't even pay attention to what he's saying. The front of the card I'm holding has a couple kissing in a snowfall. Underneath it is the name Sam and another name. One I recognized from Instagram, and scrutinized, but assured myself it was nothing. *McKenzie.* McKenzie is gorgeous, with smooth brown skin, long black hair, and eyelashes so curly and lush, it immediately made me rub my own after I peered at hers on my screen. According to her profile, she is a first-year med student at the University of Minnesota and hopes to become a pediatrician. So basically, everything I'm not, with my graphic arts job and curly brown hair that frizzes with just a touch of humidity. As I stare at the envelope, I notice my thumbnail is chipped. I bet McKenzie's fingers are always perfectly polished.

Why would Sam be giving me a Christmas card with names written on it so large? There's only one reason, one I can't even bear to think about but force myself to read lower, my heart sinking a fraction of an inch with every word I read.

I draw in a sharp breath. Under their names are the words "Join us" and the date of New Year's Eve. I jerk my head up and meet Sam's gaze. *Finally,* he's looking straight at me.

His hands fidget with the cake box, and I want to rip it out of his hands and stuff the slice of cake down my throat in defiance. How can he do this to me? And in the navy wool sweater I bought him last Christmas?

"Yeah." He's biting his lip, but his eyes sparkle with excitement. Mine, on the other hand, are definitely *not*. "It's sudden. But when you know, you know. And I recognize this is awkward, considering we broke up, but you were such a significant part of my life... and we promised to be friends, always. And I don't know about you, but I meant it. I would love to have you there as I take a big step in my new direction."

New direction? I feel like screaming. New Year, new life? Out with the old, in with the new? Sam really is as clueless as Declan always tells me he is. Especially if he takes my stunned surprise as an admission of happiness or some crap like that. Good thing he wants to become an ER doctor, not a psychiatrist, because I'd be questioning his intuitive deduction abilities right about now.

"And, of course," I faintly hear him say, even though my brain is whirling so fast his voice sounds like it's coming through one of those tinny overhead speakers you can't quite make out, "you can bring somebody..."

He looks more closely at me, probably noticing I have the facial expression of someone who just watched Rudolph get run over by a car. "I mean, are you seeing anybody?"

Am I seeing anyone? I want to scream OF COURSE I'M NOT SEEING ANYONE. How could I be, when I thought we were meeting up to get back together?

My big mouth blurts out before I can stop myself. "Yes, um, of course." Immediately, I clamp my lips shut before any more whoppers can fall out of it, like my new boyfriend is Harry Styles.

Much to my dismay, Sam's eyes light up at this bit of news. "Invite him," he urges happily.

My mouth slacks as I take this situation in, and I blink rapidly as I process it. Who actually invites their ex to their wedding? This is stupid. This is insane. This is... something I can't put up with right now. I leap to my feet.

"I'm late. For a... thing," I say. "With my, um, boyfriend. Gotta go."

Sam nods, his eyes still dancing happily. "Okay," he says. "But I'll see you at the wedding?"

Idiot, I curse him in my head. Did he really think inviting me for coffee and handing me a wedding invitation is actually, legitimately an okay thing to do? I know we promised to be friends, but friends don't pull this type of BS on one another. Especially when we broke up less than five months ago, and the wedding is in two weeks. Fourteen short days. Three hundred and thirty-six hours.

Wow, doing the math really makes it sink in further.

"Yes," I say, just to get out of there. I have no intention of going to his stupid wedding. I jerk my arms through the sleeves of my jacket and grab my purse, thanking the stars above I didn't say anything that made me sound too pathetic. The tears in my eyes did that perfectly fine on their own, thank you.

"See you and your new boyfriend on New Year's Eve!" Sam shouts out happily behind me as I run out into the cold air. "And Merry Christmas!"

Great. Wonderful. At least our interaction was so short I didn't have enough time to actually say who my mystery man is. Good thing, because he is still a mystery to me.

I almost laugh at the absurdity of the whole thing. Even if I want to go, who could I bring? Heck if I know, but if there is one thing I do know, it's where I have to go. Straight to Grandma's.

Grandma always knows what to do.

Read the rest at this link! *East Village Christmas Novellas*

Printed in Great Britain
by Amazon